Night Crawlers: "Reign of Terror"

Book 2 in a series: Night Crawlers

By

1

Ron L. Carter

Copyright 2015 by Ron L. Carter
Published at Smashwords

* * *

Smashwords Edition, license notes

This book is licensed for your enjoyment only. This book may not be re-sold or given away to other people. If you would like to share this book with another person, please purchase an additional copy for each recipient. If you're reading this book and have not bought it or purchased it for your use, only thank you for respecting this author's hard work.

***

Disclaimer

The people and places appearing in this book, as well as the story, are fictitious. Any resemblance to real people, living or dead, is entirely coincidental.

***

***

Prelude

When Jed and Chelsea left Red Mountain, they were still grieving over the recent loss of Jed's brothers, Joshua and Justin. Knowing that the Sheriff's department may also be looking for Jed, they didn't waste any time getting out of town. They only took some of their clothes and a few other personal belongings with them as they left. They then headed east toward Tennessee.

While driving, Jed voiced his anger and frustration about Joshua and Justin. He couldn't believe how violently they died. He said to Chelsea, "I'm not just angry with the people that killed them. I'm angry that they didn't listen to me when I told them not to leave the property at night."

Even though Jed didn't know what had happened between Joshua and the Sheriff's deputies, he felt like the deputies should've just captured him instead of killing him. He said, "I know Joshua didn't have a gun or any other weapon on him, so why would they kill him?" Jed had selectively forgotten that Joshua's dog, Mister, was very much a walking weapon for him during his grief. He would attack an animal or a person at Joshua's command. Chelsea tries to talk to Jed and bring him back to the reality of the truth when she says, "But Joshua did have a weapon. He had Mister. Do you remember what he did to the Mexican and the neighborhood watch guys? He had Mister kill all of them." Jed knew what she said was true but didn't want to face it. He wanted his time of grieving and anger regarding Joshua's death.

He was also angry that the neighborhood watch guys took the law into their own hands when they killed Justin. Justin didn't carry any weapon, so why would they shoot an unarmed person for just looking through a few windows? He felt the vigilante group didn't have to order to shoot first and ask questions later. Jed thought they should've captured Justin and turned him over to the Sheriff's department. He didn't feel they were justified in killing him. Although it was never said to Chelsea, Jed was glad that Joshua had killed three of the vigilante group members for their part in Justin's death. He felt some satisfaction when Joshua got his revenge.

Jed said, "They knew the dangers they faced outside our property walls. I told both that people wouldn't understand what they were doing out late at night and might try to kill them." Chelsea tried to reason with Jed, "I know, Jed, and you did everything you could to protect your brothers. They both had psychopathic behavior problems, so they didn't want to follow your orders, or maybe they just couldn't. It doesn't matter why they did what they did because they're both dead. They each had serious mental issues they couldn't cope with."

Jed lashed out in anger, "My brothers weren't crazy. Why would you say such a thing like that, Chelsea?"

She replied, "I didn't say they were crazy, Jed. I'm saying that watching someone in their home without their knowledge made Justin feel powerful. It made him feel like he was controlling those women's lives. You told me Joshua didn't feel remorse when he killed the Mexican, even after you confronted him about what had happened. You told me he seemed proud of what he and Mister had done. They didn't understand or respect other people's boundaries or the law. They never would've been able to fit in with normal society. Because of their unstable psychopathic actions, something bad was bound to happen to each of them. You couldn't protect them forever. We have to try to put all of what happened to your brothers behind us. We need to concentrate on our own family."

Jed instantly backed off from his anger toward her, and with almost a defeated attitude, he took his right hand off the steering wheel and wiped away tears with the sleeve of his shirt, then reached over and held Chelsea's hand in his.

He said, "I know you're right, Chelsea. You and the baby are all I have left in my life right now. I know I must try to forget about everything that happened to my brothers and go forward with our lives. I miss them, and it's hard."

Chelsea smiled, "Yeah, I know, Jed, but we're leaving my dad, two brothers, and all the other ugly past behind us at Red Mountain. It's just you, me, and this baby from now on."

In his heart, Jed knew Chelsea was right, and he had promised her that he would raise his kids differently from his parents, who had raised him and his brothers. He told her he would get a real job and be a good husband and father for Chelsea and the baby.

Jed never dreamed that his tangled life would make a complete circle during all his promises and eventually take him back to Red Mountain, where all the nightmares had begun for him and his brothers.

Although it was something he swore to Chelsea he would never do, Jed's tormented soul would also fall victim to a life of alcohol and drugs, just like his parents. No matter how hard he tried to fight the evil forces, they slowly took control and smothered everything good in his life. As time passed, those evil demons that once plagued Justin and Joshua would rear their ugly heads again in him and his sons.

***

Chapter 1

Jed and Chelsea had talked about where they wanted to go and decided to go to Hickory's little town, deep in the Appalachian Mountains of Tennessee. They were returning to where Jed's mom and dad were each born and raised. Jed knew that some of his mom and dad's family were still living there, and he was hoping some of them would be willing to take them in and let them stay for a while.

The day they arrived in Hickory, everything in the little town was quiet and peaceful. Chelsea loved the area and thought it was beautiful, with hills, thick brush, and tall green trees. "Why would your mom and dad ever want to leave a place like this? It's just so beautiful here; it's nothing like Red Mountain. That place is dry and hot, with no trees."

Jed laughed and replied, "Yeah, I must admit, this place is much prettier than where we came from."

He told Chelsea why his mom and dad left so many years ago because of his grandpa. "My mom said he was pretty violent with my dad, and when he got mad at him, he beat him with his fists, even when he was just a young boy. She said my dad finally had gotten enough of the beatings as he got older and decided to leave. When he left, he took my mom with him. They were both pretty young at the time. I think my mom was only around fifteen or sixteen years old."

Chelsea said, "That's just so sad, Jed. It must've been horrible for him if they were willing to leave their home and family."

As they drove through Hickory, they stopped and asked one of the store clerks if they knew the Bailey family. Everyone in the little town knew each other, and the store clerk said she knew the family well. He told the clerk he was their grandson and had just arrived from California. He soon found out from her that his grandfather had died a few years earlier from a heart attack, and his Grandmother, Bessie, still lived in the same little house where Jed's dad grew up.

One of the old-timers listening to Jed's conversation with the store clerk interrupted them and told Jed that Sherman's youngest brother, Curtis, was the only brother who never married and moved away. He still lived with Bessie and ran the Moonshine family business that Jed's Grandfather had started years ago. He told Jed that Bessie and Curtis lived in the old home place, and he gave him directions on how to get there.

Once he had the directions, Jed and Chelsea made their way down the single-lane dirt road to the secluded house at the end of the road. When they got there, Jed told Chelsea to stay in the truck until he saw what type of reception he received from the Grandma he'd never met. He wasn't sure if she would be happy or upset to see him, so he wanted to make sure before he had her get out and join him.

He slowly walked up to the front door and knocked a few times. He waited for several minutes until the door finally swung open. Standing in front of him was a wrinkled, gray-haired, robust woman. At first, she seemed a little bewildered that someone had knocked on her door. She wasn't used to getting company or anyone trying to sell something in that part of the woods. Usually, they would open the door and walk in without knocking if it were family. She was in her mid-seventies, and Jed could tell from the deep wrinkles around her eyes and face that she'd been through some hard times. From the stories he'd heard, Jed figured that maybe it was because of his Grandpa, as mean and ornery as he was supposed to have been.

Jed was nervous as he stuck out his hand and slowly said, "Hi, my name is Jed Bailey. Are you Bessie Bailey?"

She squinted her eyes and looked at him as though she recognized him as one of her kin. "Yes, I am Bessie Bailey, but who are you, sonny? I don't think I've ever met you, Jed Bailey, but you look familiar. Are you one of Jason's kids?"

Jed stuttered for a second as he tried to pour out the words. "No, I'm. I'm your Grandson, Jed, and my dad was Sherman."

Tears immediately filled her eyes as she looked at him and tried to compose herself. She believed she already knew the answer to the question she was about to ask, "Okay, so where in the heck is your dad? Did he come with you?"

Jed didn't know how to say it, so he just blurted out, "No, Dad died a few years back, but he used to talk about you and Grandpa a lot when I was growing up."

Bessie turned pale as a ghost and stepped back to catch her breath. She put her hand over her heart and headed for a place to sit. "Come in, Jed, come in. I have to sit down for a minute after you told me that bad news about Sherman. I suspected it all along but never really knew for sure."

Jed told her that he had his girlfriend, Chelsea, in the car, and she was waiting for him to let her know it was okay to come in. When she heard that, she said, "Well, for crying sake, child, have the girl come in; don't leave her in the car alone."

Jed smiled, "Thank you, Grandma. I'll go get her and have her come in." He stepped out on the porch and held the screen door open with one hand as he motioned with the other for Chelsea to come and join them.

Chelsea immediately jumped out of the truck and went to the front door. Jed had her walk-in first as they went back into the house together.

Chelsea went over to Bessie and shook Bessie's hand, "Hi, I'm Chelsea King, and I'm pleased to meet you." Bessie held both hands to her and cupped her hands over Chelsea's hand as she introduced herself and told her she was happy to meet her, too. She told them to sit on the couch while talking about everything and catching up on Sherman's life.

"You have to tell me all about your mother and father, what they were like, where they lived, and how your mom and Sherman died."

Jed began to tell her everything he could remember about his dad and mom, from when he was little until they passed away. He decided not to tell her they had both died of drug overdoses. Jed wasn't sure how she would've been able to handle that kind of news. He made up a lie and told her that they had been killed a few years earlier in a car accident, both at the same time. He didn't want Bessie to know what had happened to either of them.

Bessie asked him if he had any brothers and sisters. He looked over at Chelsea and smiled as he lied again and said no, that he didn't. Jed didn't want her to know anything about Justin and Joshua. He didn't want to try and explain to her about their deaths. It would be better if she didn't know that two other grandsons had been killed breaking the law. He also didn't want to go through trying to explain how they had a brain injury because of the drugs his mom had taken while pregnant with them.

Bessie then looked over at Chelsea and asked her if her mom and dad were still alive and if she had any brothers and sisters. Chelsea told her how her mom passed away from cancer when she was just a little girl. She also told her about her two brothers and alcoholic dad.

After a few hours of catching up on each other's lives, Jed told Bessie that Chelsea was pregnant and that they had left Red Mountain, California, four days earlier and had no place to stay. He sheepishly asked his Grandma if he and Chelsea could stay there with her for a few days. She didn't even hesitate to say, "Sure, you can stay with us, and you can stay as long as you want. You're my Grandson, and I'm happy I have this opportunity to get to know you and Chelsea. I'm happy you're with me so we can spend time and get to know each other." You can take down your dad's old room at the end of the hall." Standing up, she said, "Come on, I'll show you where it is," as she walked down the hallway to a closed bedroom door.

They had walked by another door on the way there that was also closed. "That room belongs to Curtis; it's off-limits to everyone, even me. He's your dad's youngest brother, and he never got married. He lives here with me and runs the moonshine business for us. He's cranky sometimes, but when he gets like that, all you have to do is stay out of his way and ignore him."

Chelsea smiled as she looked over at Jed and said, "We know how to do that. It's not a problem for us. My dad was like that when he was drinking."

Jed laughed and said, "Yeah, no kidding, we're used to that."

Jed left Chelsea talking to Bessie as he went to the truck, got their things, and took them into his dad's old bedroom. Soon, Chelsea joined him and started putting things away. Jed walked around the room and looked at a few old pictures of his dad while she was doing that. She laid down on the bed next to Jed when she was through. He reached over, put his arm around her, and kissed her. "Well, we can stay here if you want to."

Chelsea replied, "Are you kidding? I love it here. Your grandma seems so nice, and I can tell we'll get along just great." After talking for a few minutes, they returned to the living room and joined Bessie. They continued to speak for a few more hours.

It was getting dark when Curtis finally entered the back door and the living room. He was six foot two inches tall and a little overweight. Curtis had a belly that protruded from eating too much and not getting enough exercise. He was wearing dirty overalls over his long-sleeved shirt and pants. He had long, curly hair that stuck out on both sides and the back of the baseball cap. When he first came in and saw Jed and Chelsea, he said gruffly, "Who the hell are you?"

Jed stood up, stuck out his hand to shake, and said, I'm Sherman's son, Jed, and this is my girlfriend, Chelsea. Curtis seemed shocked as he stood there for a minute, not knowing what to say.

After what seemed like an uncomfortable amount of time to Jed and Chelsea, he shook Jed's hand and said, "Wow, we never knew Sherman even had any kids. We knew nothing about your mom and dad after they left Hickory." That's when Jed began to tell him his version of what happened to his mom and dad. Curtis said, "Doesn't surprise me. I always thought maybe he'd died somehow since he never came back." Curtis wasn't very friendly because he didn't like having uninvited guests intrude into his private space.

On the other hand, Bessie was thrilled to have her new grandson and girlfriend stay with them. She told Curtis, "They will stay with us for a while. I gave them Sherman's old bedroom; they can stay in it."

Curtis wasn't too pleased to hear that as he looked at Jed angrily, "So, how long are you planning on staying?"

As Bessie said in a rough voice, Jed didn't have a chance to say anything, "They can stay as long as they want, and I don't want to hear you say any more about it." Curtis wasn't happy, but he didn't say anything else to her about how he felt about them staying. He knew the house was still his mom's house, and he wasn't going to start a fight with her over them staying there for just a little while.

Turning to his bedroom, he said, "Just let me know when it's time to eat, okay, Ma."

Bessie smiled at them and said, "See, I told you he was rough talking, but his bark is worse than his bite." She said, "Come on, Chelsea, you can help me fix us all some dinner." Chelsea was happy to help as she headed into the kitchen with her. Jed was happy his grandma had taken them in so eagerly, so he followed behind and sat at the kitchen table.

While talking with his grandma in the kitchen, Jed told her that he needed to find a place to work until they could afford to get their home. Bessie told him that she would talk to Curtis if he wanted and tell him that he would work with him to make and sell the moonshine. Jed was surprised but happy that his grandma would be eager and willing to let him work in the moonshine business. He looked at Chelsea and asked her what she thought about that idea.

She went over to Jed and put her arms around him. She kissed him and said, "I think that would be a wonderful idea, Jed, don't you?"

Jed turned to Bessie, "Thank you, Grandma. I'd love to work with Curtis, but I don't want to step on any toes. You must ask him first to see if he doesn't mind training me in the business."

Bessie smiled, "I have to tell you a little secret, Jed. He's not the boss of the business. I am. Don't worry; he'll teach you everything you need to know. I'll make darn sure of it."

When they were all sitting down for dinner, they had just started to eat when Bessie told Curtis that Jed would work with him and help him make, sell, and distribute the moonshine. Even though they had used a few people, Curtis wasn't happy about bringing Jed into the business.

He voiced his opinion right before them, "Ma, no offense, but we don't even know this kid. He may be a lazy worker, or he may cause us a lot of problems. We don't know. Then what do we do with him? If he's family, we may have trouble getting rid of him."

Jed said, " I promise I won't cause you any problems, Uncle Curtis. I'm a hard worker, and I learn fast."

Curtis shook his head back and forth in disgust as Bessie sternly said, "It's finished, Curtis. He's working with you, and that's the final word on the matter. He starts tomorrow, and you'll teach him all the ropes." Jed and Chelsea felt a little uncomfortable that they had caused Curtis to get upset. Curtis didn't argue with his mom, even though he wasn't pleased about them staying at the house or Jed working with him.

The rest of the dinner was a little awkward for everyone. Curtis didn't say anything about the job or them staying there.

Curtis looked across the table at Jed, "Be out back at 6:00 am and don't be late, or I'll fire you."

Jed smiled, "Okay, Uncle Curtis, no problem, I'll be there, bright and early."

Jed didn't know if his grandma liked him or if she felt guilty about how Sherman had left so many years ago. He didn't care because they had to have a place to stay, and everything seemed perfect for them. Chelsea and Bessie had also started to form an early bond with each other, and he felt good about it.

Jed soon found that, even though Curtis was a nuisance to work with, he soon taught him everything he needed to know about the business, and it was easy for him to fit right in. They had quickly settled into a routine. Bessie spent all her waking moments with Chelsea and soon loved her like a granddaughter. Chelsea loved the attention she was getting from Bessie because she never had a chance to get that kind of attention from her mom. She and Bessie loved their time together.

It didn't take long, and the days turned into weeks, and the weeks turned into months. Jed and Chelsea were happy together, living there with Bessie. Every day, when Jed got home from work, he and Chelsea would sit on the couch next to each other and cuddle while watching television with Bessie. They felt like they had become part of a family.

As Chelsea came closer to giving birth, her belly was getting larger and larger, and Jed felt like she was going to pop. When he was home from work, he would tease her as he rubbed her belly. Bessie spent every day helping her prepare for the birth. Since Jed and Chelsea didn't have insurance, she had arranged for a midwife to come to her home and deliver the baby for them. Jed didn't think it was a big deal because he figured she was giving birth to a baby. He thought everything would be fine with the midwife since his grandma had recommended her.

When the day finally arrived, and Chelsea went into labor, the midwife came over and prepared everything for the delivery. Bessie was right by Chelsea's side the entire time, holding her hand while Jed was at work.

Chelsea had been in labor for several hours before Jed arrived home and soon took over his grandma. He held her hand the rest of the time she was in labor. Because it was her first child, she spent hours in and out of labor pains. Once the baby's head started to breach and was ready to deliver, the midwife told Jed to wait in the other room while she had the baby. She told him she would get him once everything was fine with Chelsea and the baby.

When the baby arrived, it was a healthy six-pound boy. Soon after that, another baby's head showed up, and it only took a few minutes, and another boy was born. It was just about the same size as the first one. They put the babies in a crib that Bessie had bought especially for them. The midwife suddenly realized something was wrong. Chelsea had a condition called Placenta Praevia, which caused extensive bleeding and hemorrhage. The midwife started to get a little frantic when she couldn't stop Chelsea's bleeding, not realizing what was happening. If she'd been in a hospital, they would've been able to give her immediate emergency treatment, but she wasn't. She was at home. Without that emergency care, it wouldn't have taken long before Chelsea would have bleed to death. The midwife tried everything she could, but she could do nothing. They immediately called the ambulance service for help. Hearing there was a problem, Jed jumped up and rushed to Chelsea's side. He held her hand and told her he loved her while waiting for the Ambulance to arrive. When they finally got there, it was too late. Chelsea had died while waiting for them.

What was supposed to be an easy childbirth and a happy time for Jed and Chelsea was another nightmare disaster for Jed. The woman he loved so deeply had given birth to two healthy identical twin boys and lost her life in the process. He was devastated by what had happened. He was shocked and couldn't believe Chelsea had died just giving birth to their sons. As he sat there, he cried out in heart-wrenching pain. She was still soaked in her blood as Jed put his arms around her. He then pulled her up close to his chest. Jed began to cry with deep sobbing emotion. The ambulance attendants just packed up their things and gave him as much time with her as he needed before putting her body in the ambulance and taking her away.

Bessie and the midwife cared for the babies while Jed tried to understand what had happened. He always felt like Chelsea was the voice of reason and the smart one between them. She always kept him stabilized when things went wrong. Now, for the first time in his life, he did feel all alone and lost without her. He cried out, "Now, what will I do, Chelsea? I don't know if I can go on without you."

Bessie had come to love Chelsea and felt like she had suffered an enormous loss when she died. She took control of the boys and cared for them like her own. Jed was lucky that his grandma immediately started caring for their every need when he couldn't. She fed them, changed their diapers, and got up with them in the middle of the night. She did everything she could for them, just like Chelsea did.

In the days after Chelsea's funeral, Jed was distraught and unable to work. He didn't get out of bed for several days and began to sink into a deep depression. After about a month in total despair, Bessie finally went into Jed's room, sat on the edge of the bed, and talked to him. She told him he had to now think of his two boys, pull himself together, and get back to work. Bessie said to him that would be what Chelsea would've wanted. She told him Chelsea would like him to be an excellent father to the boys. Bessie also told him the boys were his responsibility, and he needed to name them each and start caring for them when he wasn't working. She would help him as much as possible but wouldn't be around forever to care for them.

It took Jed a few more weeks to finally grasp himself. It took a couple more days after getting out of bed until he could eventually return to work. After a few days back at work, he came home one evening and told Bessie he'd decided to name the boys. He said that Chelsea wanted to name the baby Dalton, and if it was a boy, to call one of Dalton and Cooper.

***

Chapter 2

Jed had become like a lost puppy after Chelsea passed away. He didn't know what to do with himself. Jed left Dalton and Cooper with his grandma during the day and worked in the moonshine business. When he got home at night, he didn't know how to or want to be a father. Jed tried to spend time with the boys and take them into his bedroom while watching television. Deep down, he resented the boys because he felt they were responsible for taking Chelsea's life. Jed didn't want to feel that way but couldn't help his feelings. The more he tried not to let those thoughts affect him, the worse it became. He found the best thing for him to do was not think about them at all.

A few months after Chelsea's death, he felt lost and sorry for himself, so he started sampling the moonshine while at work. Many nights, he would come home drunk and stumbling around. He would just come home during those nights and go straight to bed without saying a word to anyone, not even his boys. He wasn't eating dinner and was getting skinny and malnourished. Bessie was worried about him and tried to sit with him and talk about his drinking problem. After trying several times, she couldn't get anywhere with him. He was hell-bent on self-destruction, and it was clear that he had become an alcoholic.

By then, she'd become very attached to the boys and feared that Jed would get angry with her for saying something about his drinking problem. She feared he would leave with them and never return, just like Sherman had done many years ago. For that reason, she didn't press him about it. Bessie allowed him to continue to destroy himself slowly. Because of her fears and insecurity, she had become his enabler.

Curtis would get upset with Jed for drinking on the job, but he knew he couldn't fight with his mom about it. Whenever he said something to her about Jed's drinking, she told him to leave him alone and mind his own business. When Bessie wasn't around, he would take jabs at Jed and say hurtful things to him when he was drunk. It caused a lot of resentment between the two of them. Jed wanted to leave and take the boys away, but he had nowhere to go.

As Jed's drinking progressively worsened, sometimes he would take off for a few days and wouldn't tell Bessie or Curtis where he was going. During those days, he would go into town to purchase some drugs. If he didn't have enough money for the drugs, he would break into a few houses and steal things to sell or trade to get the drugs he needed. He would stay high if the drugs or alcohol would last and then make his way home. He had become the person he swore he would never become.

The boys were growing up without a father. They had their great-grandmother, but they didn't have that bond with Jed they needed to help them become healthy adults someday. They were becoming like lost souls, and they might not have survived during those younger years if it hadn't been for Bessie.

As soon as they could sputter words, they developed a dialog that was all their own. Only the two knew what the other was saying, and it sounded a lot like "Parrot Talk," but it was a little different. As they got older, Bessie would ask them what they were saying, and they wouldn't tell her. They kept their communication to themselves because they didn't want anyone else to know what they were saying. Since she didn't know what they were saying, she couldn't very well discipline them for the bad things they might say. They also had the uncanny ability to understand what the other was thinking, as other identical twins sometimes do. Bessie didn't believe in beating a child, so she let them get away with a lot of trouble.

As they started getting a little older and going to school, they found they could make fun of the other kids and say hurtful things about them right to their faces in their secret language. They could do it without the kids even knowing what they were saying. After they made fun of them, they would pretend they didn't say or do anything wrong.

When they got sent to the principal's office, they would talk normally and say they didn't know why the other kids had a problem with them. They didn't like going to school and being with all the other kids. They would rather stay home and spend time with each other. They had become very antisocial and did everything with each other. They were together day or night.

When they were only six, they would make fun of Curtis and then laugh about what they said right before him. They would call him fat, ugly, and derogatory names, and he never knew what they were saying. He just knew they were making fun of him, and he didn't like it. When Curtis would go into one of his angry moods, they would laugh. They even made fun of their dad when he would come home drunk at night. They also made fun of Bessie because she was old and sometimes forgot things and part of the little game they played.

Curtis added to the problem when he would harass them by telling them they were skinny little runts and needed to eat something before drying up and blowing away into the wind. He also made fun of the way they talked to each other. He didn't like them and wouldn't back down from them when making fun of him. His anger with them had caused deep-seated hatred among the boys.

By the time they were nine years old, they had developed a sick and deadly hatred for most animals, especially cats. They were just like their Uncle Joshua, and they hated them. Something wasn't right with their chromosomes, just like Joshua. It was deeply rooted in the genetic makeup that made them the way they were, and they had no control over how they felt. When they see a cat out by itself, they throw rocks at it or chase it into the woods with sticks and try to kill it.

On one occasion, they chased a cat into the woods, and it ran up a hickory tree. They started throwing rocks at it until they hit it in the head, and it came tumbling down. While it was dazed and trying to reach its feet, they started pounding it with sticks. They beat it until some of its guts were hanging out. When they were through killing the animal, they high-fived each other as if they had just killed some dangerous beast from the forest. They were proud of themselves for killing a defenseless and helpless little cat.

Cooper thought they should return the dead cat to the old shed behind the house and burn it. Dalton went along with it because it didn't matter to him; it was just a cat. When they got home, they took the cat and put it in the old shed. They kept it hidden until the next day when they had more time to plan their move to burn it.

Staying hidden from Bessie, they got up early the following day, went to the kitchen, and grabbed a box of matches. They talked to each other in their dialog and laughed as they made their way to the shed. Once there, they took the cat's carcass and laid it on the floor on some old, dried-up newspapers. They carefully wrapped the newspaper around the mangled cat and then lit it on fire. The flames shot up like setting fire to a dried-up Christmas tree, and some newspaper on fire drifted up and caught some other papers in the shed on fire. Before they knew it, everything inside the hut was catching on fire. They ran from the shed when they realized what had happened and hid in the woods. They watched the fire as it engulfed the building. Curtis spotted the fire and ran to get the water hose to put it out. They were laughing and jumping excitedly as they watched it burn.

Curtis started fighting the fire, and the boys ran to the front of the house. They went through the living room to the kitchen. Bessie watched Curtis fight the fire from the back door, so they quickly put the box of matches back where they had gotten them and joined her on the back steps. Cooper asked her how the fire had started, and she said she didn't know. She said, "It's weird that it would just catch on fire like that because that old shed has been there for years, and nothing like that had ever happened to it." Curtis tried his best to extinguish the fire, but it was too late, and it wasn't long before the shed burned to the ground.

That night at the dinner table, Curtis had an angry look as he looked over at the boys and asked them if they knew anything about how the fire started. They had already talked about what they would say if anyone asked them, so they both said, "No sir, we don't know anything about it. We were out in the woods when it started."

Curtis looked over at Bessie and Jed and said, "You know that's a damn lie. That old shed has been there for over sixty years; why would it suddenly catch on fire without a little help?"

Bessie immediately said, "Are you saying these boys started that fire, Curtis?"

He replied, "You damn straight. I think they're the ones that did it."

Bessie said, "You can't just blame anyone you want for something like that. Do you have any proof they are the ones that did it?"

Curtis lowered his head and said, "No, Ma, but I know they had something to do with it." After that, he didn't say anything else to anyone about how he felt. Even though he believed they started the fire, he knew he couldn't win, arguing with his mom.

After dinner, when the boys went to their room, they laughed about how spectacular the fire was and how they simultaneously burned the cat and the shed. They were proud of themselves for what they had done.

Cooper said, "Did you see how fast that thing went up?"

Dalton said, "Yep, it was fast, and we were lucky to get out of there before we caught on fire, too."

When they were only ten, they visited one of their only friends to play video games. His parents were gone for the day, and the boys would be there alone. They had been there only a few hours and enjoying their day playing the games when a cat came peaking in from the other room to see what was happening with them. It was their friend's family cat, fat, fluffy, and overly friendly. It came into the room and tried to rub up against Dalton, and he quickly moved his body away from it. It did the same thing to Cooper, and he also was uncomfortable with it being so loveable and affectionate. Their friend was so busy playing video games that he hadn't noticed what was happening.

While their friend played the game, Cooper nudged Dalton with his foot and then nodded toward the cat. Dalton instantly realized what Cooper wanted to do. They smiled at each other, and in their dialog, Cooper said, "Ok, let's get it. I'll get it, and then you come and join me."

Cooper got up from the game and told his friend he had to go to the bathroom for a second. His friend was so deep into the game that he ignored Cooper leaving the room. On the way to the bathroom, Cooper entered one of the other bedrooms. He got a pillowcase from the bed, went back into the living room, lovingly picked up the cat, stuck it in the pillow, and then twisted it and tied it at the end with his belt. He took the cat into the bathroom and sat it on the floor. Thinking it might be playing a game with Cooper, the cat didn't make a sound as it just sat there. He then returned to the room and told Dalton he needed him for a second. Dalton told his friend they would return and followed Cooper to the bathroom. Dalton saw Cooper put the cat in a pillowcase and had him wrapped up tight.

They locked the door behind them as Cooper smiled and told him he would drown it in the toilet. Cooper took his belt off the pillow and laid it aside while holding the end of the pillowcase. Dalton chuckled and grabbed the other end of the pillowcase, and they submerged the cat in the toilet. The cat immediately started fighting and scratching for its life. It was useless; they continued holding it under the water until it stopped moving.

When finished with their horrendous deed, they smiled at each other, and Cooper took the pillowcase with the cat outside. He ran about a hundred yards into the woods, dumped the cat like a piece of garbage, and then ran back to the house. While he was doing that, Dalton went back into the room to finish the video game with his friend. Cooper put his belt back on and threw the empty wet pillowcase in the washing machine on his way back into place. Without a thought of any remorse, they had killed a loyal and beloved member of their friend's family.

The following week, when they saw their friend, he was angry with them and didn't want to talk to them. When they asked him what was wrong, he asked if they had killed their family cat. He said his mom and dad believed Cooper and Dalton stuffed the cat in one of their pillowcases from the spare bedroom and drowned it. When they got home that night, his mom found the wet pillowcase in the washing machine. It had damp cat hair on the inside of the pillowcase. Dalton and Cooper immediately denied doing anything to the cat, but their friend didn't believe them and told them they were never welcome at his house again. It angered Cooper, so he said, "We don't care. We went over there first only to play the video games."

When they turned eleven, Bessie began to get sick and sometimes wouldn't get out of bed until noon. The boys were pretty much on their own and had a lot of time on their hands. When they weren't in school on the weekends, they would pack a sack lunch, leave the house, and be gone most of the day. They would roam the woods to see what trouble they could find.

They could talk Bessie into letting them take out her twenty-two rifle when they went into the woods. They told her it was to kill snakes in case one tried to bite them. Bessie always told them to use it only for snakes and to avoid getting hurt. Before giving it to them, she showed them how to load it and see it on a target. She gave them several shells and told them to kill as many snakes as possible.

She didn't know they would take turns shooting anything that moved every time they went into the woods. They killed squirrels, rabbits, snakes, and anything unlucky to cross their paths. It didn't matter to them. If it were alive and breathing, they would kill it just for fun. Once it was dead, they would leave the dead animal where they had killed it. The only animal they had any compassion for was dogs. They never would harm or kill any of the dogs around town.

Bessie was in her late eighties, and her health continued to deteriorate. It wasn't long after she showed the boys how to use the gun to pass away during her sleep. Bessie was the only mother the boys knew and the only stabilizing force in their lives. They were lost when she died.

Bessie had already planned her entire funeral in advance, including the services, so Curtis didn't have much to do. All her family came to her funeral to say their last farewell. Jed's other two uncles and families were also there. Over the past twelve years, Jed had gotten very attached to his grandma and was saddened to see her go. They had talks that lasted late into the long night hours when he was sober enough to sit and visit with her. Out of respect for her, he stayed sober during the few days everyone was there and ensured the boys were on their best behavior.

Jed knew it wouldn't be long before Curtis kicked him and the boys out of the house after Bessie passed away. He never liked them living there with him in the first place. It didn't take long, only a few days after the funeral, and everyone had left. Curtis went to Jed and told him that he and the boys had to move out. He told Jed that the house was his now, and they weren't welcome under his roof now that Bessie was gone. He said he didn't want his disrespectful little brats living with him any longer. "Mom's not around to protect your sorry ass anymore, and I don't want your drunken butt around me. I also don't want your mouthy, little disrespectful runts making fun of me anymore. They don't have any respect for anything or anyone."

Jed tried to tell Curtis that the house had also become his home for the past twelve years. He and the boys had no other place to go and pleaded with Curtis to let them stay with him. Promising Curtis to stop drinking if they could stay. Curtis knew Jed could never stop drinking, but he agreed to let him work one more month to have enough money for wherever he planned to go. He told Jed he would give him that month to figure out where he was going, but that was it. "If you're not out of here at the end of one month, I'll throw your things in the front yard and lock all the doors and windows where you can't get back. I'll call the law and have them lock you out if you don't leave."

Jed knew he didn't want to get the law involved, so he kept pondering over where he and the boys might be able to go. He talked with the boys and told them that his Uncle Curtis didn't want them living with him now that Bessie was gone, so they had to find another place to live. He told them to be ready to leave in a month because that was all the time Curtis was willing to give them. The boys weren't pleased about having to leave their home. That was where they were born, and they didn't know what it would be like to live elsewhere. They hadn't even been out of the little town of Hickory since they were born.

They never really liked Curtis, and now they were angry with him for making them leave. When they had left there, they started making fun of him every day and trying to harass him in any way they could. As the days went by, Curtis got increasingly agitated each day they spent there. He wouldn't talk to Jed and tried to ignore the boys when he was home.

Jed finally sat down with the boys and told them he had no other ideas about where to go, so he thought they should return to his hometown of Red Mountain, California. He told them they would go there and see if their mom's dad and brothers still lived in Randsburg. Maybe they would let him and the boys stay with them until they could find their own place. It had been twelve years since he and Chelsea had left, and he wasn't sure what he would tell them once he got there. He knew they would be angry with him because he hadn't told them that Chelsea had died.

Jed couldn't make enough money working with Curtis and the moonshine business to have enough money to drive to California, so he started going out and breaking into houses and stealing things to sell after he got off work. The trip would take about four days, so he needed enough gas, food for himself and the boys, and three nights in inexpensive hotels.

Counting down the days before they were supposed to leave, the boys started making Curtis's life miserable. At first, they just started misplacing the things he used daily. They hid his favorite hat, his razor, and some of his work clothes. They moved his keys from where he kept them on the rack by the back door. They put Visine in his coffee a few mornings before he went to work, knowing he would be on the toilet all day.

The worst thing they did was they went out into the woods and killed a skunk. They took some of Curtis's clothes and rolled the dead skunk over them. When they finished, they hung them back up in his closet. They did everything they could think of to torment him. They continued to do it until it was time for them to pack their things and leave.

After screwing with him until he snapped, he came roaring into the boy's bedroom. The skunk smell did it, and he felt they had pranked him once too often. He lost his temper and was in a rage as he started screaming and cussing at them. He was huffing and puffing while he yelled out obstinacies and called them a few horrible names. He told them that if they were his kids, he would take a strap to them and beat the hell out of them until they would behave like normal kids. They didn't say anything; they just sat there like innocent little boys and waited for him to quit yelling at them. When he finished, they looked at each other and then laughed aloud. He was so angry with them that he just went busting back out of the room.

That night, Jed told the boys he had enough money and would leave in a few days. His patience with Curtis and what the boys were doing to him had worn thin. He told them he couldn't take being in the same house with Curtis, or someone would end up getting killed. He didn't mean he would kill him but was angry with Curtis about how he talked to the boys and how they treated him. He told the boys to ensure they had everything packed and ready to go.

When Jed told them they were leaving in a few days, the boys decided to pull one last prank on Curtis before leaving. They entered the garage the next day and got a gunny sack, a few feet of rope, and an empty five-gallon paint bucket. They found a long tree limb with a fork at the end. Once they had everything they needed, they headed deep into the woods. They went to an area with many large rocks on the side of a hill. They had found this place when they were hunting with the 22 Rifle. There were a lot of rattlesnakes hiding in and around the rocks. They decided to capture some alive and take them back to the house.

When they arrived, they could find a den full of rattlesnakes trying to stay out of the heat. They began to pull them out one at a time and put them in the bucket. When they caught twelve of them, they put the gunny sack over the top of the bucket and transferred them into the bag. They twisted it around, tied the rope at the top of the gunny sack, and then put it back in the bucket. When they caught the snakes, they talked to each other about what they would do with them.

The boys got up early the following day and waited for Curtis to go to work. They packed everything in the pickup they would take with them. Just before Jed was ready to leave, the boys told him they wanted a few moments alone in the house to say goodbye. Jed was waiting in the pick-up and didn't know the boys had gone to their closet and pulled out the bucket of snakes. They had left the snakes in the gunny sack all night and were agitated when the boys started taking them out. They put five angry and deadly snakes under the covers of Curtis's bed. They put two in his closet, where he kept his boots and clothes. They turned the last five loose in Curtis's room and closed the door behind them as they left. When they finished, they laughed and high-fived each other. Cooper said he hoped one of them would bite Curtis and kill him.

They laughed and joked around with each other in their dialog about Curtis and the snakes. Jed thought they seemed a little so happy to be leaving their home but thought it might just be the expectations of going on a long road trip, or it might even be the thought of a new place to live that excited them.

As Jed and the boys moved west toward California, it was just getting dark when Curtis got home from work that night. He walked around the house and saw that he was alone and that Jed and the boys had moved out. Jed had done just as Curtis had demanded of him and left his home. It made him very happy. He didn't have to deal with those little brats anymore. He made dinner, sat down, and enjoyed his time alone before bed.

When it was time to go to bed, he did what he always had done: he went into his room, took off his clothes, and laid them on the nightstand beside his bed. Not paying attention, he turned off the light and lifted the covers to crawl under them. His large body's weight unknowingly laid down on one of the rattlesnakes, and it instinctively turned and bit him on the stomach. Knowing that a snake had bitten him, he immediately threw the covers off and climbed out of bed. Just as he did that, he heard the rattles of another snake near his face. Winching from the pain of the first bite, he started to move out of bed slowly. The snake near his face bit him in the forehead right above his left eye just as he moved.

When he got bit by the second snake, he jumped the rest of the way out of the bed, and when his foot hit the floor with a loud thud, another snake lying next to the bed bit him on the leg. As he turned on the lights, his bed and the rest of the room crawled with snakes. When he saw them, he said, "Those little brats stuck snakes in my bedroom." When he grabbed his clothes and boots, he got bit by yet another snake near his shoes. He had just reached the kitchen to call for help when he collapsed on the floor. The last thing he said was, "Those little bastards, they've killed me."

***

Chapter 3

Hickory Dalton and Cooper were happy and excited when they left as they jumped in the front seat next to Jed. They were excited about spending time with their dad but also anxious to get out of there before Curtis got home. They didn't want him to find out they were the ones who put all the snakes in his bedroom and then told their dad.

They had a lot of time to talk to each other as they made their way to California. Jed told the boys where they went in California's high desert. He told them it was dry and hot during the summer and cold nights once the sun went down. "We are going to the three little active ghost towns of Red Mountain, Randsburg, and Johannesburg. They used to mine gold years ago, but all the miners have left. Most of the still-standing houses are the ones the miners built and lived in over a hundred years ago. There are hills around where we are going, but they don't have the beautiful trees and thick brush they have back home in Hickory. It's just miles and miles of nothing except for sagebrush, yuccas, and other desert plants." He told them they might not like their new home, but they had no choice, so they would have to get used to it. The boys knew they couldn't return to Hickory after what they'd done to Curtis.

"We are going to see if we can stay with your mom's dad and brothers for a while." He hadn't even given it much thought that Dillon and Tucker might be out on their own. Time had almost passed him by while he was grieving over Chelsea.

"They have a house in the little ghost town of Randsburg. That's where your mom grew up and lived with her dad and two brothers."

Dalton blared out, "Is there any ghost there?

Jed laughed, "That's what some of the old-timers that live there say."

Cooper blared out, "I hope I see one. If I do, I'm going to kick his ass."

Jed cocked his head to one side and raised his eyebrows as he looked over at Cooper, "You're not supposed to talk like that, Cooper. I've talked to you about that kind of language before and told you I don't like it."

Cooper lowered his head and replied, "I'm sorry, dad, it just slipped out."

Jed said, "Your mom's mother died when your mom was just a little girl, and she had to help take care of her two younger brothers.

Your Grandpa's a nice guy when he's not drinking, but he used to get drunk almost every night."

Cooper couldn't help himself as he blurted out, "You mean, like you, dad?" He then realized that was the wrong thing to say as Jed gave him an angry look but didn't say anything.

"I don't know much about your mom's brothers because we left there twelve years ago, and they were in their mid to late teens."

Dalton found his chance to speak when asked, "Was mom pretty? How did you meet her?"

Jed took a deep breath as tears filled his eyes, and his mind went back in time, "I met your mom when she worked at the bar and restaurant in Randsburg called "The Joint." She was only around seventeen or eighteen years old at the time. When I first saw her, I thought she was the most beautiful person I'd ever seen. She had a way about her that just pulled you in. She was kind and gentle, but most of all, she was beautiful. Both of you boys look a lot like her. You have light blond hair and big blue eyes, just like her. When I first met her, she was friendly and nice, and it was easy for us to talk. I fell in love with her almost at first sight, and it didn't take long before I knew she was the one I wanted to be with for the rest of my life." Dalton said, "I wished we could've gotten to know her." Jed said softly, "Me too, Dalton, me too."

Dalton asked, "So what did you guys do for fun back then."

Jed thought for a minute and said, "Your mom and I spent much time hanging out at "The Joint." I just hung out there mostly while she worked, and she would visit me when it wasn't too busy. I loved those days back then. I wished I had them back. We also drove into Ridgecrest a few times and watched a movie."

Cooper said, "That sounds pretty boring to me, dad."

Jed then told them that they had cowboy days in Randsburg every year, and it was a two-day event and a fun thing for everyone to attend. "During that time, we just hung out and enjoyed the music and the people. We also went to "Whiskey Flat Days" in Kernville and took Justin, Joshua, and Mister. We mostly enjoyed each other's company because we loved each other so much. I lived with my mom, dad, and two brothers in a little neighboring ghost town called Red Mountain.

Cooper doesn't wait for Jed to tell them about his family when he says, "So what happened to them?"

Jed hesitated to collect his thoughts and said, "My mom and dad both had a drug problem and died in their early forties from drug overdoses. It's too bad because they would've loved you, boys."

Dalton said, "I wish we could've met them, too."

Cooper asked, "So what happened to your two brothers?"

Jed stopped for a minute and tried to keep from becoming too emotional when he said, "Justin and Joshua were both a few years younger than me, and they had some serious mental issues and couldn't cope with their lives very well."

Cooper interrupted, "What kind of issues did they have?"

Jed said, "They didn't know right from wrong when it came to certain things, and that got them in a lot of trouble with people in Red Mountain and the law. They each ended up getting shot and killed. A vigilante group killed Justin from Red Mountain for peeping into houses at women. A sheriff's deputy killed Joshua after killing three of the vigilante men for killing Justin.

Dalton said, "Wow! That sucks."

Jed said, "Your Grandpa, Justin, and I used to break into houses and steal things from people in the three little towns. When Justin and Joshua got killed, your mom and I left and went back to Tennessee. That's why I tell you, boys, to avoid trouble. I don't want anything like what happened to my brothers to happen to the two of you.

Dalton said, "That won't happen to us, dad."

Jed didn't say anything, but he was hoping he was right. "When we get to Randsburg, you boys can't tell anyone what I'm telling you about your uncles or what we did. The Sheriff's department is probably still looking for me, and they would come after me, arrest me, and throw me in jail for the rest of my life, especially since I stole things in the Rand area. Do you understand what I'm telling you?" They each shook their head that they did and said they wouldn't say anything to anyone.

Jed continued telling them about the past, "Joshua had a dog named Mister. We got his mom and dad from the SPCA, and when they had puppies, Mom let Joshua keep one of them. As he grew, he kept getting bigger until he became humongous. He was scary and intimidating and could've eaten either of you with just one bite." He stopped for a minute and laughed when he said that. "Joshua trained him to do anything he wanted him to do, even kill people. He and Mister had a secret way of communicating with each other, much like the two of you do. The only thing needed to get Mister to do something was making a certain sound with his tongue. Mister would do whatever Joshua wanted him to do. He was a beautiful dog but vicious. He was a one-man's dog and wouldn't listen to anyone except Joshua."

Dalton had a severe look on his face as he looked over at Jed, "You know, Dad, we've never had a dog of our own. Do you think we could get one when we get to California?"

Jed replied, "Let's not get ahead of ourselves; we don't even know where we'll stay. Let's get home first, and then we'll talk about it.

The boys had many questions, and they continued hammering Jed with them for the next several hours while he was driving. He had gone about twelve hours when he told the boys he had to stop and get some sleep. They were happy to hear him say they were getting tired and sleepy because the excitement had worn off. They had started falling asleep while he was driving. It wasn't long, and he found a cheap hotel in one of the little towns, and they bedded down for the night. All the questions the boys had asked him brought back many suppressed memories for Jed and his heartfelt heavy that he was returning to Randsburg without Chelsea. When he thought about it, he felt sick in the pit of his stomach. He was going through all the emotions and felt like he had to have several beers before sleeping. Even after the beers, it took him a few hours to finally fall asleep that night.

The boys were up early the following day and ready to return to the road. They were anxious to get there now that they had heard so much about where they were going. Jed was a little slower at moving around because of the beers. He also knew he had a lot more driving ahead of him.

They repeated the long days of driving and staying at cheap hotels at night for the next three days, and the boys were getting a little tired of all the traveling. They had made it to Barstow, California, on the third night on the road. The boys wanted a little fun instead of cooped up in the room. They waited until after midnight, and Jed was asleep, then they snuck out to see what kind of mischief they could find. They walked around the hotel parking areas and let the air out of some tires along the way. They broke a few car windows and antennas off the cars around the hotel.

They did not find anything stimulating to do. The boys jumped the locked pool area's fence, stripped down nude, and jumped in the pool. The boys laughed and made a lot of noise when the hotel manager approached the gate and shined the light on them. He told them to leave the pool and meet him by the entrance. They quickly jumped out and put on their clothes. By then, the manager had the gate open and waiting for them. He told them he would take them back to the office, call their dad's room, and have him come down and talk.

He'd had complaints from people staying there that someone had let the air out of their tires and broken a few cars' windows. The manager figured they might be involved since they were willing to break the rules and climb the fence to the locked pool. He called Jed and told him he had the boys at the office. He asked if he would come down and talk to him about what he believed they had been doing. Jed was surprised because he never knew the boys had snuck out. He was tired and sleepy as he made it to the office.

When he arrived, the manager told Jed what he believed the boys had been doing. When Jed heard that, he asked the boys if they had anything to do with letting air out of the tires.

Cooper quickly spoke up, "No, sir. We don't know anything about what he's accusing us of doing. All we did was go for a little swim in the pool."

Sounding very convincing, Jed said to the manager, "Did anyone see my boys break any windows or let the air out of the tires?"

The manager said, "No, not that I'm aware of."

Jed replied, "Well, there you have it then. It's your opinion that they are the ones, and you don't have any proof." He stood up, "Come on, and boys were leaving." He left the manager there as they went back to their room.

When they returned to the room, Jed told the boys, "Get your stuff. We're leaving." They quickly got their things together and put them in the truck.

Jed grabbed his things and went to the truck. As he drove along, he said, "That was a stupid thing you boy did back there. You could've been arrested and thrown in jail. I would've had to pay a huge fine to keep you out." The boys didn't try to argue with their dad because they knew they were guilty. Jed said, "You sounded too convincing, Cooper, and I could tell you were lying. If you're going to break the law again, you need to ensure you don't get caught, like you boys got caught tonight in the pool. You must be a lot smarter than that. You automatically get blamed for anything else that happened around the place." That's all he said to them about it. The boys apologized for having to wake him up but thanked him for standing up for them.

Jed continued to drive until the middle of the afternoon, and they finally got to the tiny town of Randsburg. The boys had been giving him the wrong time about how dry and hot it had been since daylight. They were telling him they didn't like the looks of the place.

Cooper said, "a nuclear bomb hit this place. All the trees are gone. What happened to them?"

Jed replied, "I tried to tell you, boys! It's a desert country, and there aren't many trees around here except for the ones people plant in their yards."

Dalton said, "It's nothing like what I thought it would look like; it's ugly here. There's nothing pretty about this place at all."

Jed smiled, "Come on, boys, you have to get used to it. Some people love it out here in the desert.

Jed found Chelsea's dad's house and pulled up in the front. He sat there for a minute, fighting the emotions that were going on in his head about Chelsea. A car was in the driveway, but didn't look like her dad's old car. He was hoping they hadn't sold the place and moved away. After sitting there a few minutes, he told the boys to stay in the truck; he opened the door and got out. He was apprehensive about who he might encounter living there. He felt a little guilty that he hadn't stayed connected with Chelsea's dad and brothers as he knocked at the front door.

Chelsea's younger brother Tucker came to the door a few minutes later. He wasn't the skinny young boy he was when Jed and Chelsea left. He was heavier and looked more like a man now. When he saw Jed, he immediately recognized him, got a massive smile, and yelled out, "Jed."

He left the door open, stepped outside, and hugged Jed. He then asked, "Where's Chelsea?"

Jed bowed his head as he choked out, "She's not with me, Tucker. She passed away about eleven years ago. She died when she gave birth to our twin boys." Tucker's happy moments earlier were replaced with grief as he cupped his face in his hands, bent over, and began crying. Jed put his arms around him, "I'm sorry to give you that bad news, Tucker. I'm sorry, but I never told you what happened to her. I didn't know how to tell you that she had died. Even after all this time, I still have difficulty dealing with her death."

After he calmed down, Tucker asked Jed to come inside to talk and catch up on what had happened to Chelsea. Jed told him about the boys that were still out in the truck. Tucker walked toward the pick-up and motioned for them to get out and come in. Jed waived that it was okay to join them, and they jumped out and headed to the house. When they got closer, Tucker said, "Yeah, you're Chelsea's boys. You have that blond hair and blue eyes just like her."

He shook their hands and said, "I'm your Uncle Tucker, your mom's brother." Dalton and Cooper had smiles on their faces as they shook his hand and introduced themselves. "Your dad said you guys are about eleven years old?"

Cooper piped up and said, "Yeah, we're eleven and a half."

Tucker had them come in the house and sit with him as he and Jed caught up on what had happened in the past twelve years since they left. Tucker asked him what had happened to Chelsea.

Jed looked like he would cry as he hung his head down and said in a low voice. "We both thought she would have just one baby, but when she gave birth, she had two. She had a condition that caused her to bleed to death before we could get her to the hospital."

He didn't elaborate on using a midwife and trying to deliver the boys at home. He didn't want to try to explain why he hadn't taken Chelsea to the hospital in the first place. He had already beaten himself up over that issue a million times. After her death, he always felt guilty about not taking her there for the delivery. He believed she might not have died if he had taken her to the hospital instead of trying to have the babies at home.

Tucker said nothing except, "That must've been a terrible way to die and hard on you."

Jed said, "No matter how you die, it's never good when unexpected. It was the most devastating thing that ever happened to me. I'm still not over losing her. I loved her so much."

Tucker shook his head, "I'm sorry, Jed. I know how much you loved her and how much she loved you."

Jed started telling Tucker how Chelsea always talked about him and his brother Dillon and how much she missed them. "Chelsea always talked about returning home and visiting for a while after the baby was born. She never got that chance. She never knew that we had twin sons."

Tucker said, "That's sad. I've never stopped thinking about you and Chelsea. I missed her so much I can't even tell you how much. I tried to find you several times but didn't know where to look. I've always wanted to tell her I was sorry for ever yelling at her and acting stupid when she was only trying to help take care of Dillon and me."

Jed put his hand on Tucker's knee, "She knew how much you loved her, and she never felt bad about anything you did or said to her. She loved you just as much as you loved her."

Jed looked around, "Speaking of Dillon, where are he and your dad?"

Tears filled Tucker's eyes as he told him what had happened to them. "About two years after you and Chelsea left, Dad had been drinking heavily one day and insisted that Dillon and I go with him to Ridgecrest. He wanted to get something he thought we needed from town. I can't remember what we were going after now, but it doesn't matter. He was driving the car, Dillon was in the front seat, and I was in the back. None of us were wearing seat belts. We were traveling fast and going north on 395 when we went around a curve too fast. Dad crossed the center line and hit a car head-on. My dad, Dillon, and the guy in the other car died instantly. I spent months in the hospital recuperating from fractured bones all over my body. When I left the hospital, I returned to this old house, and I've lived here alone ever since."

Jed was shocked by the news, "Man, I'm sorry to hear that, Tucker. I know how close you and Dillon were. Sorry about your dad, too. It looks like we both have had some bad news to tell each other."

Tucker had tears in his eyes again as he shook his head up and down, and all he could say was, "Yep, I guess we did."

Jed quickly glanced around the house, and he could tell it wasn't as tidy and clean as when Chelsea took care of it. Tucker said his dad's life insurance on himself, paid for the two funerals, and paid off the house's mortgage. The auto insurance helped him get a new, used car to replace the wrecked one. He told Jed that he could lie about his age and get a job at the military base in Ridgecrest when he was only eighteen.

"I've been working there almost ten years, and I make enough money to take care of myself very well," Jed asked him if he ever got married, and he told him that he hadn't, but he had a fiancé named Amber. He said that she's a dental assistant and has her place in Ridgecrest. "We're getting married in about a month. We've agreed that I'll move in with her when we get married, and then I'll rent this old house out."

Jed immediately saw the opportunity and asked him how much the rent would be for the house. Tucker said, "I don't think I can get much for it, maybe $300.00 to $350.00 monthly."

Jed replied, "The boys and I don't have any place to go, so if you'd be willing to rent it to us, I'll get a job and make sure I pay you each month."

Tucker smiled, "I'm at Amber's house about three or four nights a week right now, so why don't you stay here until I get married, and then we'll talk about the rent? I don't know if I want to charge you anything for rent, Jed. You're my family. The boys can take Dillon's bedroom, and you can take dad's old room."

Jed was very excited as he reached over and shook Tucker's hand, "That sounds like a plan to me, Tucker, thank you very much. We weren't sure where to stay once we got here. I wasn't even sure anyone still lived here."

Jed told Tucker not to tell anyone who he and the boys were because of his horrible history in Red Mountain before he left. Tucker knew what he was talking about and agreed he would keep his mouth shut about him and the boys. He then showed the boys to their rooms. When they brought their things in from the pickup, Tucker started the barbeque and threw some burgers on the grill. Although he was devastated by the news of Chelsea's death, he was excited that her boys could call family.

After dinner, Jed knew he had to ask a dreaded question that had nagged him since he left Red Mountain. He looked Tucker in the eyes and said, "Do you know if the law is still looking for me?"

Tucker replied, "Not recently." Then he thought back for a minute as he replied, "the Sherriff's department a couple of times contacted us right after you and Chelsea first left. They were looking for you then, but I haven't heard from them in the past ten years since I've been here alone."

Jed was relieved to hear that news when he said, "That's great. Hearing that takes a huge load off my mind."

***

Chapter 4

A few days later, Jed checked around Ridgecrest and got a job working for Mario Florio at an auto repair shop. He would try to pay Tucker for the rent even though he wasn't asking him to. He was good with engines, and he needed to work to pay the bills and keep up with his alcohol and drug addiction.

After being in Randsburg for a few days, the boys decided to walk around town and learn more about where they would live. When they talked to Jed about it, he told them to make sure they didn't say anything to anyone about who they were. He told them that if anyone asked them questions about where they lived or were from, tell them their dad rented the King house here in Randsburg from their Uncle Tucker. He told them to stay away from the tweakers who lived in some shacks and mobile homes. "They could be dangerous if you rubbed them the wrong way.

Cooper said, "Don't worry, dad, we'll stay away from everybody, and we won't talk to anyone either."

The boys decided the first place they wanted to see was "The Joint." That's where their mom and dad first met, and they had heard a lot about the place. When they got to the old building, it was empty and locked. They didn't think it looked anything like what they had imagined. They tried to peek through the windows but couldn't see inside. A few people were driving around town, but not much was happening. The city was quiet and dead except for a few tweakers hanging out around their places.

The boys were already beginning to hate living in the desert, and they let Jed know precisely how they felt about it every chance they got. They felt like they were living in a dungeon of hell. It was so hot they felt like they could hardly catch their breath during the day, and it would get cold enough at night that they had to wear a sweater or light jacket. Because it was so hot during the day, they started going out after it cooled down a little in the evenings.

For the next few weeks, the boys spent their time reviewing the three small towns and checking everything out. Because of their frustration, they broke into some old empty houses. They wanted to see if there was anything they wanted to destroy or steal. They broke a few windows in the homes, and they vandalized them in some way.

Their frustration continued to mount until one day. They decided to burn one of the old historic houses that had been standing for over a hundred years. The house was part of the town's history because its first mayor lived initially. They didn't care about that; nothing about history meant anything to them. They could've cared less. To them, it was just an old ugly old house, and they wanted to burn it.

They snuck out of the house one night after Jed passed out on the couch. They took some old newspapers and a book of matches and headed to the empty house. They broke in at almost midnight and quickly set it on fire. Once it was on fire, they found a hiding place across the street where they could watch it burn. They were excited as they laughed and high-fived each other as the neighbors tried vainly to extinguish the fire. By the time the firefighters got there, it burned to the ground. Jed never found out that they were the ones that burned it down. He was oblivious to what the boys were doing around the towns. He was too consumed with his demons.

When summer was over, Jed told the boys they had to attend school. He figured it would give them something to do with themselves during the day while he was working. Based on age, they were supposed to be in the eighth grade, but they didn't go to school as much as they should've when Bessie was alive and responsible for getting to school. When school started, Jed took them and dropped them off. He told them they had to use King's last name on the way there because if they used Bailey, the Sheriff's department might figure out who he was and come after him.

The first week the boys were there, they appeared to be very friendly and likable to all the other kids and teachers. They acted like and seemed normal eleven-year-old kids in every way. Even though they appeared to possess charming personalities, they were just manipulative to everyone at school so they could gain their trust.

The second week they were in school, they figured they didn't care. They got into several fights with some of the other boys. The boys were making fun of how they dressed and talked because they were from Tennessee's backwoods. They had developed the southern drawl and spoke much differently than the California kids. Fitting in with these kids was more challenging than anything during their years in Tennessee. They felt like the other kids were attacking them.

Everything changed for them during that time, and their survival instincts started to kick in. They fought back without wanting or willing to conform to their current social environment. They developed the attitude that they weren't part of the school group and never formed a social attachment to the kids or the teachers.

They spent a lot of time at the principal's office during that second week. When Friday rolled around, they were suspended from school for one week for fighting. When Jed went to pick the boys up from school, the principal had him come into her office and talk to her about them. During their conversation, she told him that she felt the boys suffered from a lack of social connection to the rest of the kids and had no respect for the teachers or authority. Jed wasn't surprised by what she said because they had already retreated and didn't let anyone else in.

When he left the school, Jed was angry with what the principal had told him. After getting in the car with the boys and on the way home, he didn't know how to handle the situation, so he yelled at them, "I told you, boys, to stay out of trouble. What's wrong with the two of you? Why won't you listen to me? Don't you understand you could get me in big trouble if you have to go to the Juvenile Detention Center? I'd have to go down there to the place and try to explain to the police who you are?" He didn't realize it at the time, but the boys hadn't spent time in Juvenile Detention because they had become very clever at hiding their criminal activity. He seemed more focused on what might happen to him than the boys' welfare.

Cooper spoke, "But dad, the kids at school have been making fun of how we talk and dress. It's happened every day since we started that stupid school."

Jed replied, "It doesn't matter. It would help if you boys learned to ignore their insults, or you'll get in trouble every day you're there. I don't want to be called into the principal's office like that again. Do you boys understand me?" They continued to try to tell Jed that they didn't feel like they fit in with the other kids at school, but he wouldn't listen to their excuses or anything they had to say.

Then, the boys decided they wouldn't talk to anyone at school and tried to ignore what the kids said. They would use their dialog with each other when the other kids were around. They would start making fun of the kids like they used to do with Curtis. After doing that for a few weeks, they found they could make fun of the other kids, laugh at them, and get away with it.

Soon, they became the misfits and outcasts of the school because of their behavior and inability to fit in. Because they were so willing to fistfight the other boys, the other kids developed fear and tried to stay away from them. They wouldn't include them in any activity or have anything to do with them. The boys had to eat by themselves and spend all their time together. Even the teachers had developed a fearful and stand-offish attitude toward them. They also wouldn't ask the boys to participate in school activities because they would fight with them or the kids.

After the first month of school, the principal had Jed come in again and talk to her about the boys and their inability to fit in with the teachers and other kids. It angered Jed because he felt like the teachers and the other kids had isolated themselves from the boys, not the other way around, as she claimed. Jed told her they would talk about everything once they were home. He never spoke to them about what the principal said because he felt better about them not being so friendly and social with everyone. He felt it kept them isolated and his identity safe, and he was okay with that.

Despite everything the principal had said to him, Jed got up every morning and took the boys to school. He wanted them to get an education and would drop them off on his way to work. That was usually the only time they spent together. He worked long hours at the shop and got home late at night. He was so busy that he didn't control what they did once they got home from school.

They were supposed to ride the bus home every day after school until one day when they got kicked off for fighting with the other kids again. After that happened, Jed forced them to walk home every day. When Jed found out about it, he said, "You deserve to walk home because you didn't do what I told you to do and stay out of trouble." They tried to explain what had happened, but Jed refused to listen. "I don't want to hear your excuses. If you don't want to follow the rules, you have to suffer the consequences of your actions."

The boys had a lot of time on their hands every day before Jed got home at night. They didn't have anyone to watch over them or try to guide them in the right direction. They had to fend for themselves. They were deprived of the right food and nourishment because they had to fix their meals. That just added to their frustration and anger. They were living in poverty, which added to the breeding ground for some of their criminal activity. Jed had become a stranger to the boys, and they didn't feel he cared about or loved them. Because of their frustration, when they talked to people, they became very disrespectful to everyone, including Jed.

Over the next few years, the boys continued to develop the "bad kid" attitude. They did everything they could to torment the people in and around Randsburg, the neighboring Red Mountain, and

Johannesburg towns. The boys would hide and throw rocks at passing cars and houses. They would break windows out of people's houses when they didn't think anyone was home. They stole things people left out in their yards and killed several family pets in and around the towns for fun. They had a total lack of disrespect for other people's personal property and authority. Nobody could catch the boys in the act of committing any crime, so that they couldn't report them to the police. They were extremely good at hiding the things they had done. The town people knew they were troublemakers and had developed a deep dislike for them. They hated to see the boys come around.

They were sitting around bored one day, so they decided to explore all the abandoned mines they could find in the area. They went out and spent the entire day hunting for the different mine locations. While studying, they encountered a few Western Diamondbacks and Mojave rattlesnakes. Jed had told the boys about the snakes in the desert because of what happened to Justin. He told them, "It's sometimes hard to tell the two rattlesnakes apart because they both have diamond shape patterns. The difference is that the Mojave rattlesnake is greenish and can grow up to four feet long. The Western diamondback has a white line that extends from the eye to the mouth and can grow up to seven feet long. If it's nighttime, you can tell the difference when you come across one. They both sound the same. If you get bitten by the Western Diamondback, it might not kill you, but the Mojave rattlesnake is more aggressive than the Western Diamondback, and if you get bitten by it, you could die if you don't get to the hospital in time. You must stay clear of all the snakes if you can because they are both venomous, and you don't want to get bitten by either one of them." Usually, the boys would pick up huge rocks and smash the snakes in the head, so they never had a problem with them.

When they discovered the mine near the old Silver Dollar Saloon, Cooper wanted to go to the bottom of the old mine shaft and explore what was down there. It took the boys a while to scrounge up enough rope to tie it together to get to the bottom. They carried it down to the mine shaft and tied it around a massive boulder near the hole. They dropped the rope into the hole and waited for the sound of its end hitting the bottom.

Cooper told Dalton, "I'll go down first and check it out, and then when I come up, you can go down and check it out yourself."

Dalton said, "Why don't I go down with you, and we can explore it together?

Cooper looked at Dalton like he was stupid and said, "Somebody needs to stay at the top, just in case something goes wrong, dummy."

Dalton wondered what could go wrong but went along with Cooper's statement.

They had brought a couple of flashlights to look around once they were at the bottom. Cooper stuck one of them in his back pocket as he grabbed the rope with both hands and started descending. When he got about three-quarters of the way down, the string came apart where they had tied it. Cooper fell the rest of the twenty feet to the bottom. He landed with a thud, which knocked the breath out of him at first. Dalton was yelling down into the hole and asking if everything was alright. There wasn't an answer for a few minutes because he was still trying to catch his breath. Dalton started to panic until Cooper finally yelled back up to him that he was okay.

Cooper yelled to Dalton, "The rope must have fallen where we tied it. You'll have to go back home and see if you can find some more rope. If you can't find any at home, try to borrow some from somebody. You can tie it to the rope's end when you find some, and I'll climb out of here. Try to hurry because it's creepy down here."

Dalton yelled to him, "Okay, I'm going to throw the other flashlight down and see if I can find more. I don't know how long it'll take, so relax and return as soon as I get it." He dropped the flashlight into the hole before running toward the house.

The second flashlight busted apart when it hit bottom, but Cooper could shine a light on it and retrieve the batteries. While waiting for Dalton to return, Cooper started looking around at everything down, realizing that he had landed in the middle of a few skeletons and a couple of skulls. After shining the light on the bones, Cooper quickly pushed himself away from them. He stood up and, looking around, realized there wasn't much else to see interested him. It wasn't long before he started getting bored with being down there and wanted out.

When Dalton returned to the house, there wasn't anyone home, so he frantically looked through the tool shed and everything else, trying to find more rope. Not having any luck, he went to a few neighbors to see if he could borrow some from them. None of them were willing to help him because of all the bad things the boys had been doing around town. After trying several people, he realized it was no use; none of them would help him. Dalton would have to wait until his dad got home and see what they could do. He knew his dad kept a long rope in the pick-up for emergencies.

Cooper had been in the hole for over four hours before losing the light from all the batteries. He wondered what was taking Dalton so long and started to get nervous about being down in the hole. Dalton should've been back hours ago. Sitting in the dark with the skeleton remaining, he started to freak out a little. Cooper began yelling and hoping someone might hear him. Not getting any response, he finally gave up, sat down, and waited.

Waiting for Dalton to return, he felt scared as he imagined hearing the laughter from the ghosts down there as they made fun of him. He also suspected he could hear them say, "You'll be down here with us for a long time, boy. You might as well get used to it, but don't worry, we'll take good care of you." He tried to put his hands over his ears so he couldn't hear what was happening in his mind. That didn't help because he could still listen to what he thought were their voices. Being down there started getting to him, slowly driving him crazy.

It was late when Jed got home, and Dalton ran out to meet him in the driveway. He immediately told his dad what had happened. Jed had a seven-five-foot rope in his pick-up, so he told Dalton to hop in the truck. Cooper had been in the hole for almost six hours when they arrived. Once there, Jed yelled down to see if he was alright. When he heard his dad's voice, Cooper was both relieved and apprehensive as he said to himself, "Oh crap, now we're in big trouble. Dad's going to kill us for this." After a short hesitation, he told his dad that he was okay. Jed pulled up the rope, tied it to its end, and threw it back into the hole. He asked Cooper if it reached the bottom, and as Cooper grabbed hold of it, he yelled back to his dad that he had it. When he had a good grip, he climbed up the rope until he escaped the hole.

Once he was out, Jed pulled up the rope and wrapped it around his shoulder. While throwing it in the back of the pick-up, he growled, "What the heck was you, boys, thinking by going down in that place?

Cooper looked at him with a gloomy, sheepish look, "Sorry, dad, we were looking for something to do, and it seemed like a good idea then. I'm sorry that we had to bother you with this."

Even though Jed was angry, he was relieved that Cooper wasn't hurt when the rope came loose, and he fell the other twenty feet to the rocky bottom. "Don't do something stupid like that again. The next time, you may not be so lucky." They both said okay, which was all that Jed ever told about. He didn't even ask Cooper what he had seen while he was down there. Maybe because he already knew the answer to a question like that.

Before they went to bed that night, Dalton asked Cooper how things went down there in the old mine and if anything was interesting to see.

Cooper said, "Nothing but bones and skulls and a couple of creepy ghosts that kept laughing at me."

Dalton laughed aloud and said, "Yeah, that's funny! I thought you were tough, and you would beat it up if you ever saw one."

Cooper hit Dalton on the shoulder, "We'll, that was the problem. I didn't see them. I just heard their creepy voices."

By the time they were thirteen years old, things had gotten a little out of hand with them. Some people in Randsburg knew Tucker called him on the phone and told him he had to do something about the renters living in his house. They believed the boys were causing much trouble in the Rand area. He tried to make excuses for them until the calls became too frequent for him to ignore.

He finally had to talk with Jed and tell him what everyone in Randsburg said about the boys. He said he was getting a lot of pressure from the people in town and would have to move. "I need to sell the house anyway. There's no reason to keep it now that I'm married." He told Jed he would give him forty-five days to find another place to live.

Jed spent the next few weeks looking around the three towns to see if he could find a place they could afford to rent. During his search, he went by the old house in Red Mountain where his family lived. It still looked the same, except for a few missing tins in the fence and weeds around the decaying old house. There were signs on the property from the Bureau of Land Management saying, "no trespassing." Jed wondered if they would be willing to rent the old house to him and the boys. He also asked himself if he could live in the place after what had happened there.

Not being able to find anything else available he could afford or that would rent to him because of the boys, he finally mustered up enough nerve to go to the Bureau of Land Management to talk to them about renting it. When he sat down with the person in charge of the property, it was an older man with solid gray hair and a beard by Clyde Snow's name. When Jed introduced himself, he gave Clyde the name of William King and asked him if the place might be for rent. Clyde looked at him weirdly as he squinted his eyes, "You are talking about the old Bailey House?"

Jed pretended to be dumb, "I'm not sure. Is it that place with the tin fence around it, and it has your signs up all around? If that's the one you're talking about, then yes, that's the one."

Clyde said, "You must not be from around here, are you, son?"

Jed replied, "No, It's my two boys and me from Tennessee, but we've been renting my cousin's house in Ransburg for a few years. He decided to sell the house, so now we need a place to live. I thought we'd check on that old place to see if you'd rent it to us."

Clyde squinted, "Well, William, I don't know if you know it, but that house has some awful history attached to it." He then told Jed about how Justin and Joshua died there. He also told him about all the bodies buried on the property law enforcement agencies had dug up. Jed pretended it was all new to him as he sat and listened. After telling the entire story and some rumors, he looked Jed in the eye, "Are you sure that you're still interested in renting that old place after hearing what I just told you?"

Jed laughed, "Yes, sir, The boys and I aren't afraid of a few old ghosts."

After talking for over an hour, Clyde finally agreed to rent Jed the house for only a few hundred dollars a month. Jed had promised him that he and the boys would clean the place up and work on the house to get it back in shape in return for the cheap rent. Jed was happy but somewhat apprehensive about returning to the house and all the memories he would have to face with his ghosts.

They were very excited when Jed told the boys they would be moving into the house where he grew up in Red Mountain. They were even more excited when Jed said he would take them down to Palmdale and see if Johnny Jackson still lived there and if he had any puppies from Mister's bloodline. He figured if he had any dogs left, he would try to convince Johnny to sell him a couple cheap or maybe give the boys one.

Jed told them it would take a lot of work to get the house back in shape before they could visit Johnny. He told them they would have to help him clean the yard, repair the fence, cover-up gravesites, and work on the house. They were more than willing to do their part because they wanted their place and a dog. While they worked on the area, they talked about different names for their puppy. Dalton liked the character Skeeter, but Cooper liked the name Samson. They would flip a coin to see what they would call it once they had one. They were highly intrigued and fascinated that Joshua had trained Mister to kill anything he wanted him to kill. The boys talked about it and wondered if they would do something like that with their dogs.

They worked on the place almost daily and cleaned it up while still living at Tucker's house. Jed was still working at the repair shop, working only on the house when he had time off. Working around the house was hard because all his family memories started haunting him. The first night they were there, he felt like he could almost see and feel Justin and Joshua's presence as he went from room to room, rehashing old memories of better times when they were all together. It caused him to sink a little deeper into his despair. Working in the place caused him to drink and take more drugs to cope with all the deep emotions he was going through. The boys discussed it and hoped Jed would live there without going off the deep end.

After a short time, the boys had done an excellent job cleaning the property of all the weeds and trash and covering the empty graves sites. They also patched up the places in the fence that had missing pieces. They removed everything in the house: old furniture, clothes, and anything else left. They dug a hole in the back of the house and burned it while Jed was at work. After a few weeks of working on it, they could move in. They didn't have any furniture, so they slept on the floors in sleeping bags. Even though it was empty, it was still their home, and they liked it there.

***

***

Chapter 5

Just like he had promised, Jed left work the following Saturday after they had moved. He picked the boys up, and they headed to Palmdale to see if Johnny still lived there and was home. Even though it had been almost fifteen years, Jed could find the place without trouble. When he pulled into Johnny's yard, everything looked the same, except the grass was a little taller, and some weeds were scattered around the property.

He told the boys to stay in the truck while he went to see if Johnny was home. As soon as he got out, he heard the familiar sound of the dogs barking from the metal building outback. He instantly knew it was still Johnny's home as he looked back at the boys and gave them thumbs up.

Just as he started knocking on the door, Johnny opened it. He stood there for a minute, trying to figure out who was calling on him.

After a few seconds, he said, "Jed, is that you?"

Jed laughed, "In the flesh, Johnny." He hollered out, "Well, I'll be damned. I haven't seen you in a Koons age." He moved in closer and gave Jed a huge bear hug as he said, "Come on in, boy. You must tell me what you've been up to all these years."

Jed thought Johnny still looked the same as when they last saw each other, except he was a lot older-looking and had a few deep wrinkles. The hair on his head and beard was gray now, and he no longer had the ponytail.

Jed said, "I have two boys now, and they're out in the truck. I wanted to make sure you still lived here before I had them get out."

Johnny laughed, "This is my home, and I'll probably be here until I die." He told him to get the boys out and join them. Jed stepped away from the house and waited for them to arrive.

As they approached the house, Johnny said, "Twins, huh? Now, you boys are some good-looking dudes." He went over, put his arms around their shoulders, and headed toward the front door. Cooper quickly moved away, but Dalton thanked him for the compliment and kept walking. The boys tried to be cordial during the introduction, but they had only one thing on their minds, and that was the puppies. They were anxious to find out if Johnny had any and if he would be willing to part with a couple of them.

When Cooper first met Johnny, he felt uncomfortable with him and how friendly he was toward Dalton. He didn't like how he looked at the two of them, feeling it was a little weird to him. After they entered the house, Cooper pulled Dalton aside and said in their dialog, "Did you see how that weirdo looked at us? He was checking out our butts like we were a couple of girls or something. There's something weird about him. We better keep our eyes on him."

Dalton said, "Come on, Cooper, don't be like that. It's probably just your imagination. He seems just like a friendly old man to me."

\

Johnny went to the refrigerator and grabbed a beer for himself and Jed. They sat on the couch, and Jed told Johnny about Chelsea and how she had died when the boys were born. Jed said they lived in Tennessee for quite a while but moved back to Red Mountain a few years ago.

"We moved back when my Grandma died, and my uncle didn't want us there anymore."

Johnny replied, "That sucks."

Jed told him, "We just moved into where my folks lived in Red Mountain." By the time they were through talking about it, they each had about three beers.

As they sat there and listened to the conversation between Jed and Johnny, the boys started getting a little antsy as Cooper looked over at his dad and said, "So go ahead and ask him."

Jed then began to talk to him about the dogs, "Do you still have the fighting dogs like you used to? When I got out of the truck, I heard some dogs barking back, so I assumed you were still fighting them."

Johnny smiled as he told them he had a couple to let fight occasionally. He said, "My main guy is Cobra, and he's so mean and tough that not too many people will bet against him." He laughed and proudly said, "He's one of Mister's offspring, and he's never gotten whipped in a fight. I've won a lot of money with him over the years."

That gave Jed the perfect opportunity to speak up, "That's one of the reasons we came to see you. I promised the boys I would get them each a dog, and I wondered if you may have any of Mister's bloodline puppies available. I'm willing to pay you for them if you have any."

Johnny got excited, "Is that right? Do you think these boys could handle a couple of those mean critters?" He looked over at Dalton and gave him a wink as he said that.

He said, "Come on, I want to show you guys something." He headed out the back door and straight to the metal building that Jed remembered. The boys quickly followed behind them with eager anticipation. When they got inside, he showed them his prizefighter, Cobra. He said, "This is the guy I was talking about; ain't he a beauty?"

Jed instantly saw the resemblance to Mister; he had a muscular body and a firm stance. He looked mean and harsh, just like Mister had looked. His color was solid black except for a white muzzle and white on the tips of his toes. He had deep white scars around his face and head from some of his previous fights. He was built just like Mister, only a little smaller in stature. Jed said, "Man, I can't believe how much he looks like, Mister. He's not quite as big, but still a beautiful dog."

Johnny then motioned for them to follow him to the pen at the end of the building. When they walked over and looked down, he laughed aloud as he pointed at six clumsy puppies and the Staffordshire bull terrier mother wagging her tail. She was pitch black, with no other markings on her. She was firm and intimidating-looking. Johnny said, "Don't let that scary look bother you, Jed. She's as gentle as a lamb. She wouldn't hurt a human being for anything in the world. Now, another dog is a different story."

He told them the puppies were seven weeks old and starting to get around independently. "That's the mom, and Cobra is the dad. That is one heck of a combination, wouldn't you say?"

Jed replied, "Those will be beautiful dogs when grown." Johnny said, "I'll give each of the boys one of them if you think they can take care of them. I will give the boys each one because they are from Mister's bloodline, and you were responsible for me having that." He had also instantly taken a liking to Dalton. He looked at Dalton and smiled, "Just pick out which one you boys want, and it's yours."

The boys were excited as they studied the puppies for several minutes while Jed and Johnny looked at some of the other dogs he had in pens. They finally settled on the ones they wanted. Dalton wanted the male puppy that was completely black, except for a white mark on its chest, and Cooper wanted the male puppy that was completely black, like its mother.

When Johnny returned, they told him which ones they wanted, so he went into the pen, got them, and handed them to the boys. He put his arm around Dalton while he was holding the puppy. He ran his fingers through Dalton's hair and said, "There, your dog's now, boys. You'll have to feed, water, and take care of them." They were so excited about the puppies that they didn't pay too much attention to Johnny and how he was so overly friendly. He had made the boys very happy with the gifts he'd given them, and Jed didn't overthink how Johnny acted.

Dalton told Cooper when they went outside, "See, I told you he was just a nice old guy." Cooper just mumbled a few words to himself and kept his mouth shut. He already had formed his opinion about Johnny and didn't want to argue with Dalton. He only wanted to take his puppy and get out of there as quickly as possible.

They hung outside playing with the puppies while Jed and Johnny returned to the house and had a couple more beers. When the boys returned to the place, Jed told them they would be spending the night.

He told them that Johnny was good enough to offer some hamburgers to barbeque, so they might as well relax and enjoy themselves. They knew their dad had a few too many beers to drive them back to Red Mountain safely, so they were okay with spending the night.

Johnny entered the kitchen and pulled out an old coffee can hidden under the sink. He took out a hundred-dollar bill and returned the can to its hiding place. Johnny handed him the money and said a convenience store was just down the street. Cooper had been watching Johnny intently and knew where he stashed his can full of cash. Johnny said, "Why don't you go and get us some more beer and grab a six-pack of soda for the boys while you're at it."

He looked over at Dalton, smiled, and said, "Is there anything else you boys might want while your dad is at the store?"

Dalton said, "No, sir, we're good." Cooper said, "Yes, how about some chips to go with the burgers and cookies?"

Johnny showed the boys where they would sleep while he was at the store. Jed thanked him and took off to the store. Johnny's kindness was starting to wear on Cooper. He felt like it was all just some kind of an act to make his move on one of them. He believed he knew what his real motives were. Jed had left the boys vulnerable with a man he hardly knew. He might have thought he knew him, but that was long ago.

Once Jed went to the store, Johnny took the boys into a two-bed bedroom. He pointed to one of the beds in the corner of the room and said to Dalton, "You take that one, Dalton and Cooper; you can take the other one." Jed had already agreed that he would sleep on the couch. Dalton was still holding his puppy, so Johnny went over, petted the puppy, and hugged him. He had his arm around him, saying, "Look at that little rascal. He loves you already. You must be special, just like him. What are you going to name him?"

Dalton looked up at him and smiled, "I'm going to call him Skeeter.

"Johnny said, "Cool, that's a good name. I like it." In Cooper's opinion, Johnny continued to be overly friendly to Dalton and didn't like it. He just thought Johnny's behavior was a bit too bizarre for him.

It wasn't long before Jed returned with the beer and handed Johnny his change. He thanked him for being so kind and gracious to him and the boys as he opened one of the beers for each of them. After a few more beers each, Johnny started cooking the burgers, and the boys were starving. They each gladly gobbled down a couple of burgers, chips, cookies, and a couple of soda cans.

Before they went to bed, Cooper whispered to Dalton, "You better grab a butcher knife from the kitchen and stick it under your pillow because I don't trust that guy. He seems too strange to me."

Dalton said he was crazy, "Relax, Cooper, we'll be out of here in the morning, and we got our dogs. That's what we came for, and that's all I care about."

Cooper replied, "Yeah, you're right. I should keep my mouth shut about him." They laughed about it and high-fived each other before they went to bed.

Cooper was trying to trust his institution about Johnny, so he stayed awake until Dalton fell asleep. He snuck into the kitchen when his dad and Johnny weren't looking. Cooper pretended to be just getting a glass of water. He found a large butcher knife from one of the drawers and a hammer from a toolbox under the sink. Not caring what Dalton thought, he took them and put them under his pillow for their protection.

In the middle of the night, Jed is passed out on the couch when Johnny tries to take advantage of his opportunity. He came staggering into the boy's bedroom and didn't have any clothes on from the waist down. He went to where Dalton was sleeping, sat on the edge of the bed right next to him, and woke him up.

Once he was awake, Johnny whispered, "Hey Dalton, you want to have a little fun? Dalton was still half asleep and confused about the question. He sat there for a minute, trying to wake up, and didn't answer. Not getting a response from Dalton, Johnny took it as a positive sign, so he reached down between Dalton's legs and tried to rub his private parts. Dalton quickly slapped his hand away.

Johnny said, "Come on, you don't have to act like that. I'm not going to hurt you." By then, Cooper and Dalton were wide awake, and Dalton couldn't believe Cooper was right about Johnny.

Dalton yelled out for his dad, but Jed was asleep and didn't hear him. Johnny got a little irritated that he did that, so he became a little more aggressive as he tried to put his hand over Dalton's mouth. "Don't worry about your dad. He's asleep, and this will be our secret. Nobody has to know that we just had a little fun with each other. Besides, he doesn't care about you boys anyway. He wouldn't be lying drunk on my couch if he did."

Those words cut through Cooper like a knife to the heart. He instantly felt the blood rush to his face as his body tensed up, and he grabbed his weapons. While Johnny directed his attention at Dalton, Cooper quickly slipped out of bed and stood right behind him. He had the hammer in one hand and the knife in the other. Seeing that Johnny wasn't backing down from his intentions with Dalton, Cooper took a full-round house swing with the hammer and hit Johnny as hard as he could in the back of the head. There was a loud crunching sound as the hammer crushed Johnny's skull, and his body instantly stiffened out.

To Cooper, it seemed like he was in slow motion as he fell off the bed and onto the floor. His body then started kicking and jerking like he was having a convulsion. He lay there shaking for a few minutes while the boys watched in total shock. It wasn't long before everything with Johnny stopped moving, and he lay there like he was dead.

Cooper laughed nervously and said, "I told you something was weird about that guy. He was going to rape you if I hadn't killed him. Do you believe me now?"

Dalton was still a little shaken by everything that had happened and shrugged his shoulders, "Yeah, ok, you were right, and I was wrong. What will we do with him now that you've killed him? We have to wake dad and tell him exactly what happened." Cooper didn't want to tell his dad about it, but they had no choice. He knew his dad would find out in the morning when he woke up, and then he would be even angrier with them for not telling him sooner.

They went over to where Jed was sleeping and started to shake him violently until he finally woke up. Once awake, it took a few minutes for him to get his baring. He was startled and still drunk as they began to tell him what Johnny had tried to do to Dalton. When Johnny tried to grab Dalton by the penis, Cooper hit him across the head with a hammer and killed him. Listening to their story, Jed thought he was in a bad dream and that what they told him wasn't real.

After several minutes of telling him what happened, they finally took Jed by the hand and led him into the bedroom, where Johnny's half-nude body lay next to the bed. Once he saw Johnny in that position, he knew what they told him was true. He was trying desperately to make sense of it because that was the last thing he had ever expected from his friend Johnny. He thought he knew him well and believed he could trust him. In Jed's drunken state, he tried to figure out what they should do and never checked to see if Johnny was dead. He just took the boy's word for it, and that's who he was. He didn't know or even realize that Johnny was still alive and breathing.

For a moment, Jed yelled out, "Oh My God. It can't be happening again." He told the boys to go back to the equipment shed and see if they could find a couple of shovels.

Dalton asked, "What will we do with him, dad?

Jed replied, "We're going to bury him just as we did with the Mexican when Mister killed him." They hadn't heard that story before, but now wasn't the time for him to try and explain it to them. Even in his drunken state of mind, he knew there was no way they could report this to the police. He knew he would've ended up in jail, and the boys would've gone to the Juvenile Detention Center.

Jed went to an area of the property and believed he found where they had buried the Mexican so many years ago. He told the boys they would bury Johnny next to him and showed them where to dig. Jed told them to dig a hole about six feet deep and wide enough to throw Johnny's large body. They searched for about an hour until he told them that was good. While they were digging, Jed was taking that time just trying to sober up enough so he could drive back to Red Mountain once this nightmare was over.

When the hole was deep enough, they all went back into the house and got Johnny's body. Jed was still drunk and didn't check to see if he had a heartbeat or was breathing. They carried him to the hole and dumped him in it. Without any hesitation, they then covered him with dirt. Once finished, they put leaves and rocks over the top to camouflage the new grave. They took the shovels and put them back where they found them.

Jed went into the house, wiped his fingerprints off the beer bottles, and threw them in the trash can outside. He also wiped everything he felt he and the boys might have touched, including the hammer that Cooper had used on Johnny. Jed told the boys to grab their puppies and meet him in the truck. Cooper told Dalton to hold his puppy for him because he had something to do before leaving. Dalton ran into the bedroom and grabbed the two puppies, while Cooper went to the kitchen and snatched the hidden coffee can full of money.

As he drove back to Red Mountain, Jed felt he'd returned in time. It was as though he was driving along with Joshua and Justin again. He felt like he was in slow motion as he made his way back home. Just before they got home, Cooper pulled out the coffee can full of hundred-dollar bills.

Jed was surprised to see the can full of money, "Where did you get that?"

Cooper replied, "That pervert had it stashed under the kitchen sink. I watched where he hid it when he gave you money for the beer."

Jed told the boys to start counting it and see how much was there. Johnny had stuffed all his betting money in that old can, and there were over ten thousand dollars in it.

Jed believed it was the money Johnny used when he would go out and fight his dogs. Jed would never have agreed to keep the cash if Johnny were still alive, but he figured it was their just reward because of what happened. He finally laughed aloud, saying, "Well, since he doesn't have any use for it anymore, I guess we'll be able to put it to some good use. Maybe we can get some beds and other used furniture, maybe even some new clothes for all of us. Thank you, Johnny. We appreciate the gift." They all laughed aloud together as Cooper and Dalton high-fived each other.

Jed had thoughts of anger, confusion, and frustration going through his head just before they got home. He used to like Johnny and never knew he had any pedophile problems. Driving along, he felt he had to ask Cooper one question before they got home. He looked over at him, "So Cooper, how do you feel about killing someone for killing Johnny?"

Cooper chuckled and replied, "I feel good about killing him, and he deserved what he got. He was a piece of crap, a pervert. He probably would've raped Dalton if I hadn't killed him." Dalton didn't say anything; he just shook his head up and down and agreed with Cooper. Jed rolled his eyes and tried not to get mad or figure any of it out.

Deep inside, his heart screamed, "I can't believe I'm going through this again, just like I did with Joshua. My boys are killers." He would never know because he was too drunk, but he was the natural killer. He had the boys bury Johnny while he was still alive and breathing.

***

Chapter 6

Jed called in sick to work and stayed home with the boys for a few days to try and wrap his head around what had happened with Johnny. While off work, he and the boys went into Ridgecrest to one of the used furniture stores and spent some of Johnny's money on beds and other furniture they desperately needed for the empty house. Jed believed this was just what they all needed to make a fresh start at the old place. While in town, they also bought some new clothes for each other. They spent almost half the money from the coffee can and put the rest away for safekeeping.

When Jed returned to work, he started dropping the boys off at school, as always. They discussed it before school and decided to ditch it when Jed dropped them off. Once his truck was out of sight, they hid from the school officials and returned home. When the school officials reported it to Jed, they ditched school for a few months. He was angry and frustrated that the principal didn't let him know immediately. From then on, he decided he wouldn't fight the boys about school. He knew he couldn't make them go if they didn't want to, and he couldn't be with them every minute of the day to ensure they did go. He also knew the teachers and the students at school didn't like the boys, so he wondered why he should make them go if they weren't welcome there.

When the boys had been ditching school, they spent time with Skeeter and Samson. They were going through the tedious work of teaching the puppies how to respond to their commands. They didn't use the dogs' names to get their attention; they used their dialog to train them in what they wanted them to do. They had certain sounds they made for every command they wanted them to follow. They wanted to make sure their dogs wouldn't listen to anyone except them, just like Mister wouldn't listen to anyone except Joshua.

They first taught the puppies not to jump or chew on either of them while working with them. They used a treat reward system with the dogs to make them listen, giving them a lot of positive reinforcement. It was a slow process and a lot of constant repetition, but after only a few months, they were able to teach the dogs to sit, lie down, roll over, fetch, heel, go to the bathroom outside, and not bark or growl unless given a specific command. Everything the dogs did had a particular order the boys used just for them.

By the time the dogs were four months old, they had taught them how to attack and grab a weapon from someone. For more advanced training, the boys got muzzles for the dogs and practiced striking the two of them. They taught them how to go for the throat when attacking a human. By the time they were six months old, they were each over sixty pounds and still growing. The way they grew, they would be well over a hundred pounds each once developed.

After months of training the dogs to follow their commands, they practiced with dummy animals. They wanted something more exciting to do with them. It was like someone with a new guy who couldn't wait to use it. They tried to find out how the dogs would react to killing a real live animal. Cooper told Dalton, "Having these dogs is like having a bike in the garage and not being able to ride it. We have to find out what they can do."

They soon devised a plan to take the dogs out of the property to see what they could find and kill. When Jed came home from work, he usually drank several beers or took some drugs until he passed out on the couch. After Jed passed out, they took advantage of their opportunity and started taking the dogs out at night.

Some paths connected the towns, and the locals used them for years. The trails were about four feet wide and worn clean from all the foot traffic over the years. Not many people used them after dark, so Dalton and Cooper felt safe going out at night. They took the dogs and stayed on the paths where it was easier to travel during the night.

They began hunting for any animal they could find, searching for food or a mate. Sometimes, it was a rodent, a squirrel, or a stray dog or cat. The dogs stayed right by Dalton and Cooper's side and didn't move or make a sound when hunting until they got a command to attack. By the time they were eight months old, they had turned into vicious killing machines. When they spotted an animal, it very rarely got past them.

At first, the dogs were awkward and slow when they attacked the animal, but the boys were patient and repeatedly worked with them. They started having the dogs attack from different angles to cut off the escape route their potential victims tried to take. That made it easier for the dogs to catch their prey together. One would go after the animal, and the other would cut off its escape route. Once they killed the animal, the boys left it where it was mauled to death. It was a gruesome sight, with guts and body parts lying around most of the time. By the time they were eight months old, they had turned into vicious killing animal machines.

They took their dogs out as often as possible without getting caught by Jed. When they tired of killing the animals in Red Mountain, they decided to move on to Johannesburg and finally to Randsburg. It wasn't long before many people in the three small towns complained about losing their pets. Some believed there might be a couple of young mountain lions on the loose that were killing them, especially after they saw how their animals had been ripped apart and then just left there. People started carrying guns when they went out at night, only in case they spotted the animals.

It was like any other hunting night for them when the boys took the dogs to Randsburg. They heard a dog barking in the distance, so they decided to head for the sound. They saw a border collie outside its fenced-in yard when they approached the barking dog. It was standing in the middle of the road and just barking.

Cooper chuckled and whispered, "Look at that stupid dog. He's not barking at anything at all. He seems to be barking just to hear himself bark."

Dalton sneakered and whispered. "Big mistake for him."

The boys had the dogs move into position, one from the left and the other from the right. The dogs stayed hidden in the sagebrush as they crawled within about ten yards of the dog. By then, the dog had spotted them and gone a little crazy. When the time was right, Cooper commanded them to attack. The dogs immediately jumped from their hiding places and charged toward the dog. They both hit him almost simultaneously and instantly had him on the ground, ripping on him with their strong jaws and sharp fangs. The dog was yelping, growling, and trying to fight back, but he was no match for the overpowering dogs. It only took a few minutes, and they ripped his body apart.

Once the dogs had killed their intended target, the boys commanded them to heal. The dogs instantly stopped what they were doing and returned to Cooper and Dalton's side. Each boy said, "Good boy," and patted their dogs on the head and back. The dogs were panting hard, and their tongues hung out as they occasionally lapped it back in and looked up at their masters. They stood there like proud warriors and excited about what they had done.

Cooper and Dalton were also excited. They had already gotten back on the trail and were heading home. A man came out of the house from where the dog lived. They had only gotten a short distance from the house, and the dogs noticed someone was following them. They each let out a low growl when they spotted the man. He was about two hundred yards behind them, moving fast as he jogged in their direction.

They stopped for a second and looked back as Cooper told Dalton, "You take the dogs and get ahead of me, and I'll stay back and see what this guy is up to. When everything is okay, I'll catch up with you."

Dalton said, "Ok, I'll meet you at the crooked bend in the trail." It was about a half-mile from where they were.

Cooper waited for the man following them to come along the trail, and then he stepped out in the open and started walking toward him.

Cooper could tell he was in his mid to late forties and was carrying a rifle when he got closer. His hair was messy, like he'd just gotten out of bed. When Cooper first approached him, the guy stopped, took careful aim, and was ready to shoot him.

Cooper quickly raised his hands and said, "Hey, Mister, don't shoot me. I'm unarmed."

The guy could tell Cooper was probably a high school kid as he growled, "What the hell are you doing out here all alone at night? Haven't you heard that some animal is killing our pets around here?"

Cooper played it cool and said, "Yeah, I heard that too, but I was just heading home from my girlfriend's house in Red Mountain."

Still angry, he asked Cooper, "Did you see the guy on the trail with a couple of large dogs?"

Cooper replied, "All I saw was a guy walking his two dogs. Is that what you're talking about?"

"Did you see what he looked like?" he asked.

Cooper replied, "I couldn't tell much. It was too dark. Maybe in his thirties, but he had two big dogs with him."

The guy replied, "Yeah, I think those two big dogs killed my dog. I saw them as they left my house, so I followed them to see where they went." Cooper realized that he and Dalton were in big trouble with this guy. He knew he couldn't let him find out about them and where they lived. If they got caught, they would go to jail to kill all the animals around the towns and, worse, trouble their dad. The police might even find out their last name was Bailey and not King, go after their dad, and put him in jail.

Cooper said to the guy, "My name is Cooper. What's yours?

He shook his hand as the man reluctantly stuck out his and said, "I'm Donald Pickens, and I live back in Randsburg."

Cooper said, "Come on, Mr. Pickens, I'll go with you and see if we can catch up with that guy and his dogs. We'll find out if they were the ones that killed your dog." Cooper turned and started back in the direction of Dalton.

Donald said, happy to have the company, "If we hurry, maybe we can catch up to them. I'll put a bullet in them both for killing my dog. I may even shoot the owner for letting it happen."

Cooper was angry that he was willing to shoot someone he didn't know. Even though he could feel the blood rush to his face, he kept calm and calmly replied, "I don't blame you, Mr. Pickens. I'd kill him if he let his dogs kill my dog."

As they walked along the trail toward Dalton, he asked Cooper where he lived and who his girlfriend was. Cooper told Mr. Pickens he lived in the old King residence in Randsburg. As soon as he said that, it hit Mr. Pickens, and he realized Cooper was one of the twins, causing a lot of trouble around the towns.

He said, "Hold on there a minute, son; I know who you are now. You and your brother are the ones that have vandalized the empty houses and caused a lot of other trouble around here."

Cooper was very good at lying, saying, "You must have me mixed up with someone else, Mr. Pickens. I don't even have a brother." Cooper was very believable as he denied everything Mr. Pickens accused him of doing. He then turned around and headed in the direction of Dalton. Mr. Pickens reluctantly followed behind him.

When they were almost at the bend in the trail where he would meet up with Dalton, he told Mr. Pickens that he had to stop for a minute and take a leak. He said, "You go ahead, Mr. Pickens; I'll catch up with you in just a minute."

Mr. Pickens didn't know what to do because he wasn't sure if Cooper was the bad kid or lying to him about everything. It didn't matter; he wasn't going to shoot an unarmed kid just because he thought he was one of the boys from Randsburg.

Cooper stepped off the path, pretending to go to the bathroom, when he bent down and grabbed a rock about the size of a grapefruit.

He waited until Mr. Pickens was about ten yards ahead of him, and then he made the sound for Skeeter and Samson to attack. When Mr. Pickens turned back to ask him what kind of sound he had made, both dogs hit him hard from behind almost simultaneously. They knocked him to the ground, and his rifle flew from his hands, flying in the air. Mr. Pickens immediately flipped over on his back to try and fight them off.

Samson had him by the throat in just a few seconds, and Skeeter had grabbed him over his face and on both sides of his cheeks.

Cooper moved in closer while Mr. Pickens was struggling to get free. He smiled as he looked down at Mr. Pickens and said, "You should've stayed home, Mister Pickens. It would be best if you hadn't been out alone at night. You were right; my brother and I were causing all the trouble around these towns, and today isn't your lucky day."

While the dogs were holding him down, Cooper hit Mr. Pickens with the rock with three hard blows to the head. He then gave the dogs the command to kill. It only took a few more seconds, and he lies dead and mangled on the path.

Dalton had come running up while the killing was going on, and he had a frightened look on his face. "What did you do, Cooper?

Cooper said, "Relax, Dalton, that guy was going to shoot you and the dogs when he caught up with you. He told me so himself."

Dalton said, "Ok, so you killed him before he killed us? Now, what do we do with this guy's body?"

Cooper replied, "There are only two things we can do. We either have to carry him back to the house and bury him without Dad finding out about it or drop him in that old mine shaft down behind the old Silver Dollar Saloon. What do you want to do?"

Dalton thought about it briefly and said, "Let's take him to the mine shaft. If dad wakes up and finds out what we did, he'll be angry. He might kill us himself."

Dalton picked up Mr. Pickens' gun, then Dalton took his feet, and Cooper grabbed him under both arms. They had the dogs stay alert if someone else might come along on the path as they carried him to the mine shaft. They took turns switching positions until they made it to the hole. They didn't waste any time as they quickly heaved his body over and down the deep drop. They waited until they heard the thud of his body as it hit bottom and then threw his rifle in after him.

When they finished, Dalton said, "We better get back. It's getting late. I don't want dad waking up and finding us gone."

Cooper just agreed with him as they headed back home.

When they got home, Cooper was lying on the bed, laughing about everything that had happened that night. He told Dalton, "You should've seen the look on Mr. Pickens' face when Samson had him by the throat, and Skeeter had him by the face. He looked like his eyeballs were going to pop out of his head. It was a funny-looking sight."

Dalton said, "You're sick, Cooper."

Cooper smirked, "Yeah, I might be sick, but I'm glad we killed that guy before he killed you and the dogs." He told Dalton that he was happy they had gotten away with killing him without anyone seeing what they had done. He figured nobody would ever find out it was them, so he was very pleased with himself.

About a week later, Jed came home from work and told the boys what he'd heard from some people in town. He told them a family man who lived in Randsburg by Donald Pickens had gone missing for about a week. His wife said she and her husband were sleeping when they heard something attack their dog out in front of the house. Mr. Pickens grabbed his rifle, loaded it, and went to see what was happening. She said that was the last time she ever saw him. She found their family dog lying dead in the gravel road out in front of the house, and he looked like some wild animals had ripped him apart.

To Jed, her story seemed eerily like what happened with Mister when Joshua took him out to kill cats and other animals in Red

Mountain many years ago. People in the towns were saying the same thing then as they are now. After hearing some of the stories, the entire thing started adding to Jed. He knew what the boys had been doing with their dogs and knew they were training them to kill. He didn't want to believe they were killing all the pets around town, but he knew in his heart that it was true.

He looked over at the boys with an angry, mean look, "I know you've been training those dogs of yours to kill, and that's what Joshua did with Mister. Those dogs are big and strong enough to kill a man, especially if they team up easily. You know something about what happened to that dog and Mr. Pickens, so you must tell me now." He threw some things on the floor and yelled at them, "Have you been taking those dogs out at night and killing animals?"

Cooper immediately spoke up, "No, sir. We haven't been doing that."

Dalton sat there with a sheepish look and didn't say a word. He was feeling very uncomfortable about Jed questioning them.

Jed looked over at Dalton and was familiar with the squirming and feeling guilty attitude Dalton was going through. Joshua had acted the same way when Jed first asked him if he and Mister were killing the cats in the area. Cooper lied to him, so Jed directed his following questions to Dalton. He got right in Dalton's face, "Did you boys have anything to do with that dead dog and Mr. Pickens? If you did, you had better tell me, or your dogs would be at the dog pound tomorrow morning. Do you understand me?"

Dalton couldn't bear the thought of losing the dog he'd trained and had become so attached to. He immediately started to speak up as Cooper tried to intervene and say something.

Jed said to Cooper, "Sit down and shut up. I don't want to hear from you right now. I want to hear what Dalton has to say."

Dalton spoke very slowly and quietly, and Jed could barely hear him. "Yes, dad, we do know what happened to him."

He then began to tell Jed the entire story about how they would sneak out at night once he passed out on the couch and how they had trained the dogs to kill other animals. He told him about how the dogs had killed Mr. Pickens' dog, and then Mr. Pickens followed them with a gun and was going to kill them. He told him the dogs attacked Mr. Pickens and killed him while following them along the trail. He said Cooper also hit Mr. Pickens in the head three times with a rock to make sure he was dead before the dogs mangled his body. Jed screamed, "So what did you do with Mr. Pickens' body after you killed him?"

He could hardly hear Dalton as he replied, "We dumped his body in the old mine shaft behind the old Silver Dollar Saloon. We also threw his rifle in with him."

After hearing the story, Jed had to sit down because he felt his knees buckle as he backed away from Dalton. He couldn't believe what he was hearing. That was what he and Justin had done with the Tweaker's body that Justin had killed on the same trail years ago. He felt like he had just gotten out of a fight as he softly and calmly said, "Did anyone see what you boys did?"

Cooper tried to speak up and say something, and Jed told him to shut his mouth. "I'm not happy with you, Cooper. You lied to me and shouldn't have lied to me about what happened. You should've told me the truth when I asked, just like Dalton did. You know I hate a liar." Cooper shut his mouth and didn't say another word.

Dalton continued, "No sir, we were cautious not to let anyone see us, and the dogs didn't hear or see anyone either." Jed was so angry that he didn't know what to do. He told the boys to go to their rooms and told Cooper that he would be in a lot more trouble if he did anything to Dalton for telling the truth. On the way to their bedrooms, he told them he might take the dogs to the SPCA the next day and have them put to sleep.

As he sat alone, Jed relived the nightmare that night so many years ago with him, Justin, and the Tweaker. He couldn't believe what Dalton had told him. It reminded him of how much Dalton and Cooper were like Justin and his unremorseful behavior. He shivered from head to toe as he tried to make sense of it. Jed had to believe what Dalton told him about killing Mr. Pickens to keep him from killing them. If he couldn't convince himself that's what happened, he would have difficulty accepting what they had done. There was no way they could turn them over to the law. They were also his flesh and blood, and he knew he could never do something like that. He had to figure something out with them before it was too late. If he didn't do something drastic with the boys, he would lose them forever, and he didn't want them to end up dead, like Justin and Joshua.

***

Chapter 7

That night, after they went to bed, Cooper was angry with how his dad had treated him when he told him to sit down and shut up. He felt like his dad was playing favorites with Dalton and didn't want to listen to anything he had to say. Jed didn't want to talk to him after he lied about everything that had happened. Cooper was also angry that Dalton quickly gave up all the details about what they had done to Mr. Pickens to his dad. He now felt sad and all alone, except for Samson. The emptiness Cooper was feeling was eating at him. He became more agitated with his dad and Dalton as he lay on the bed thinking about everything. There was no way Cooper was giving up his dog. He left the house, got as far away from his dad and Dalton as possible, and never returned.

He waited until they were both asleep, took Samson, and slipped out the back door. He was so upset and angry when he left that he wasn't thinking straight. He didn't have a plan about where he was going once he got there. He just started walking east and never looked back. He didn't even think about taking any food or water with him. He just wanted to get as far away and quickly as possible.

Cooper left easterly from the house and crossed highway 395 as he and Samson continued their trek through the desert. He crossed down and around the mountain and stumbled along, talking to himself the entire time he walked. Before realizing it, they were deep into the desert, and it was starting to get daylight. He had traveled over forty miles before he finally stopped and looked around. Once the sun came up, there were hills in all different directions, and they all looked the same to him. At that point, he realized he was lost and didn't know how to get back to Red Mountain. He sat down and panicked for a few minutes because he wasn't sure how to go. He tried to figure things out, but he knew one thing was for sure: he didn't want to go back home and have to give up Samson. He knew he had to head toward one of the hills to the east, or he would go in circles and wind up dead. He finally picked one of the mountains off in the distance and started walking in that direction.

He and Samson continued walking the entire day and couldn't see any sign of another human being. They occasionally saw a few snakes, jackrabbits, and other rodents, but no people. By dark, they were starting to get thirsty and hungry. In his haste to get away from home, Cooper hadn't even thought about bringing a pocketknife, matches, or anything else that could've helped him survive in the desert. Now, they were all alone and facing the possibility of dying out there. He told Samson, "Okay, boys, we're going to walk all night or until we can find our way out of this desert." Samson looked at him as if to say, "Okay, Cooper, I'm with you, so just get me out of here alive."

They continued walking until the middle of the night when Cooper finally spotted a dim light a few miles off. It gave him a glimmer of hope as they headed straight for it. It took him almost thirty minutes to finally get close enough to see that a light was on in front of an old, run-down shack. It was out in the middle of nowhere and miles from everything. The light was from a solar light that stayed on all the time.

When they got close to the shack, a prominent German Sheppard spotted them and started running toward them. It was barking and acting like it had never seen another person before. By the way, it was working. Cooper figured it hadn't seen many people far out in the desert. It wasn't long before an older man came rushing out of the house with a rifle. Cooper was happy and relieved that someone was home.

When he got close enough to the shack, he yelled to the old man, "Hey, mister, I'm lost and don't know how to get back to town. Can you help me?" By then, he was only about forty yards from the shack, and the older man's dog was close to him, barking, growling, and going crazy. He had to reach down and pat Samson to calm him, "Easy boy, it's ok."

To Cooper's surprise, the old man said in a deep, angry voice, "Stop right there, sonny, turn around, and go back where you came. You're not welcome here."

Cooper wondered, "What the heck's up with this guy? I need a little help. I haven't even asked him for anything yet."

Cooper didn't say anything; he just stood there and looked at the older man for a minute. The guy continued in the same voice, "If you don't get out of here right now, I'll shoot you right where you stand."

He was shocked by how the old man treated him, but he calmly replied, "I'm sorry, mister, I don't mean you any harm, but I don't know which way to go to get back to town. My dog and I can't find our way in the desert, and we're thirsty and hungry. Can you at least give my dog some water and me?"

The old man pointed his gun at Cooper and, with an even more threatening and stern voice, said, "I'm not going to tell you again, boy; now get the hell out of here, or you're going to have one of my bullets to swallow, and then you won't have to worry about water." Cooper could tell he was serious, so he decided he wouldn't argue with a guy with a gun pointed at him. He sounded serious about him and Samson leaving him alone, or he might use that gun.

Not wanting to fight with the older man, Cooper had Samson heal as they turned around and headed back in the direction they'd come. Cooper and Samson took cover in tall sage bushes once they had gotten about a quarter of a mile away. After sitting there a few minutes, he thought about how the guy had treated him and knew they might not make it out in the desert if they had to be out there another day without water. Cooper started to get angry that the older man was unwilling to give them anything before sending them on their way. The more he thought about what that older man said about shooting him, the angrier he became. Cooper wouldn't let him get away with treating him and Samson that way. He waited and watched for several minutes until the older man finally went back into the house before he decided to make a move.

While looking back at the shack and watching the older man, Cooper devised a plan. He decided he would get water from that house one way or another. He wouldn't die out in the desert because that older man refused to help him.

He took Samson and circled behind the dark side of the shack. When they got closer, the older man's dog spotted them and ran toward them, barking and growling again. This time, he seemed braver because Samson hadn't attacked him when he'd gotten close to them earlier. Cooper waited until the dog came close enough, giving Sampson the command to attack. He immediately ran, hit the dog full force, and knocked him to the ground. Sampson was ripping at the dog's throat as it yelped out in pain and tried to fight back. He gave Sampson the command to kill, and within a few minutes, Samson had him by the throat, and the dog was soon lying dead on the ground. He then had Samson heal, and he immediately ran back to Cooper and stood by his side.

Hearing all the commotion from his dog, the guy came running out of the house again with his rifle. This time, he had a flashlight in one hand, and he was shining it all around and calling for his dog. He had just reached the back, where his dead dog was lying when Cooper and Samson went the other way to the front door. Once there, they quickly slipped inside the house.

Cooper glanced around and saw that the little shack only had two small rooms and didn't see anyone else around. The place had a kitchen, a living area, and a bedroom. He ran to the kitchen area and started looking for a weapon, knife, hammer, or something. He had to have something. He grabbed a huge butcher knife from one of the drawers. It had a nice thick handle and a blade about ten inches long at the end. He told Sampson to sit as he waited just inside the front door for the guy to return.

He didn't have to wait long as he came stomping back in, yelling and cussing. As soon as he opened the door and stepped in, Cooper didn't say anything to him as he thrust the knife deep into the upper part of his stomach to the handle. When he bent over from the pain, Cooper grabbed the rifle from him with his left hand, pulled the knife out, and stabbed him again.

The old man had fallen to his knees, and just before he fell to the floor, Cooper said, "You should've been nicer to my dog and me. All we wanted was a little water and a few directions. Was that too much to ask?" He took the big, long, bloody knife and made one slash across the guy's neck, and the blood started spurting out onto the floor. Cooper pushed the rest of them away to the floor. He quickly turned around to make sure there wasn't anyone else in the house.

Not hearing or seeing anyone, he slowly crept to the bedroom entrance. He almost couldn't believe his eyes when he saw a young girl about his age cowering in the corner of the room. She had her back to him, and Cooper could tell she was shaking with fear. She was only wearing a dirty old nightgown, but he could tell she was frail and skinny, and her light brown hair was long and stringy. He thought it was odd that she had her face cupped in her hands and just standing in the corner of the room. He went over to her and was ready to stick the knife deep into her back because he didn't want to leave any witnesses to what he'd done. She suddenly turned around and looked at him, and that's when he saw the duct tape across her mouth. He also noticed that she had a chain around her tiny wrist. She was chained, so she could only get to a make-shift bathroom and back. Cooper said, "What kind of sick crap is this?"

At first, Cooper was confused by what he saw, but it all made perfect sense after a few seconds. That's why the guy didn't want him to come into the house; he had an unwilling sex slave chained to the bed that he didn't want him to see. He asked her if anyone else was in the house, and the girl shook her head, no in fear. Her eyes looked bugged out, and she was crying. He could tell she was terrified of him and the older man.

Cooper chuckled and said, "You no longer have to worry about that old man. I killed him." He laughed, saying, "Now me, that's a different story. I haven't decided what to do with you yet." Happy that the guy was dead but now fearing Cooper would kill her, she put her hands to her face and began to sob.

He left her standing there for a few minutes as he checked out the rest of the shack to see if she was telling him the truth. Once he was sure they were alone, he went to a counter and found a half-full bucket full of water. He gorged himself and then gave some of it to Samson. He washed the guy's blood off the knife and his hands from the water in the bucket.

Cooper returned to the bedroom and ripped the duct tape from the girl's mouth. He told her that he wouldn't hurt her, but she had not to scream and answer some questions for him before he set her free. He asked her who the guy was that he had killed.

She slowly spoke, "His name is Charley, and he kidnapped me when I was nine. He's had me chained to this bed ever since that day he took me. He's been raping me whenever he wanted to ever since he brought me here. When he heard you outside, he put the duct tape over my mouth so I wouldn't scream. He told me that if I took it off and screamed, he would kill you and me both."

Cooper squinted his eyes and yelled, "That sick, crazy bastard. I'm glad I killed him."

She cried as she continued, "I lived with my mom and dad when he grabbed me. I was riding my bike alone on the street."

He could tell she was telling him the truth as he asked, "So how old are you now, and what's your name?" She seemed embarrassed and shy as she softly said, "My name is Ashley Stevens, and I think I'm fifteen. I don't know for sure. I lost track of time over the years." She raised her voice, "That sick old man just called me Candy."

Cooper was stern, "Look, if I set you free, you have to promise me you won't turn me into the police for killing him. I don't want to go to jail for killing a sick old man like that."

She said, "You don't have to worry about that. I'll be grateful to get set free and go back home. You don't have to tell me your name or anything if you don't want to."

He ignored her when she said that and asked if they had a car or truck they could take to get out of the desert. She told him the guy had a pick-up truck, and he kept the keys somewhere over by the door. Cooper went to the door to look for them, and they were hanging from a nail on the wall. Once he had the ring of keys, he took them back into the bedroom. Ashley looked at him pleadingly, "One of those keys on that ring will unlock this lock and set me free."

Cooper tried a few different keys until he found the right one. While doing that, he said, "Do you know how to get back out of this desert because I'm lost, and I don't."

She replied, "I think so. That guy took me to town a few times over the years. When we went into town, he always told me he would kill my family and me if I tried to escape. He said he knew where my family lived and would kill them if I tried anything. It's a narrow, winding dirt road that winds long until you come to one of the main paved roads. Then you can take the main road to Ridgecrest."

He unlocked the lock from her wrist and said, "If I set you free, don't do anything crazy." He half chuckled, "I don't want to have Samson over there, chew you up."

Ashley said, "You don't have to worry. I promise I won't do anything. I'll be happy to get these chains off me." Cooper looked down at her wrist and saw a ring worn deep around her entire wrist from years of having the chain attached.

"You have to stay with Samson and me until we get you back to Ridgecrest, and then we'll try to find your mom and dad's house and see if your family still lives there."

She shook her head up and down and began to sob aloud when Cooper unlocked the chain. Once she was free, she immediately hugged him and said thank you. That startled him for a moment because he wasn't expecting that. He wasn't used to anything like that. He didn't realize how pretty she was until she was close to him. The last time he had gotten a hug like that was from his great-grandma Bessie before she died. When she hugged him, he told her his name was Cooper, and he lived in Red Mountain.

He asked Ashley if she had any other clothes she could throw on instead of wearing. She told him the guy had bought her a few things to wear over the years, and she could put something else on. She seemed shy as she turned her back to Cooper again and took off the old nightgown. He told her that he and Samson hadn't had anything to eat in a few days, so while she was dressing, he went over to the kitchen area and grabbed some things they could eat on the way out of there. She threw on a top, pants, and shoes while Cooper was in the other room.

Before leaving the shack, he cleaned his fingerprints from everything he had touched. They left Charley lying where he'd killed him and went and got in the truck. They headed down a small, winding dirt road toward town. Cooper had never driven a car or truck before, but he'd watched when his dad. From watching him, he had a pretty good idea of how it worked. It took a few minutes to get used to the steering and brakes of the truck. Once he figured it out, he was fine. They stayed on the minor dirt road for about twenty miles until they finally hit a paved road. From there, they were able to head to Ridgecrest.

Ashley had memorized her old address when she was held captive, so it didn't take long to find the street she had lived on and her family's house. Before they got there, Cooper wished her luck with everything. She had tears in her eyes as they got close to the home, "I'll always be grateful to you, Cooper. You saved my life. Thank you for everything."

She reached over and gave him another big hug and a kiss just before she jumped out of the truck and headed for the house.

Cooper could tell she was nervous as she walked up and knocked on the door. It was still dark outside, but the streetlights were on. She looked back at him sitting in the pick-up, and he smiled back at her and gave her a thumbs up. After several minutes, her mom came to the door in her nightgown.

She seemed shocked when she recognized her daughter, "Ashley, is that you? Ashley screamed out, "Yes, mom, it's me."

Her mom immediately started screaming and crying. While hugging each other, she turned back again and looked at Cooper. She smiled and then gave him the thumbs-up sign. Seeing that she was okay, he then headed back toward Red Mountain.

Cooper knew he would be in big trouble when he got back home, but at that point, there was no other place he would rather be. Just before he got back to Red Mountain, he wiped his fingerprints from the pick-up and found a hiding spot for it in a deep, secluded ravine about three miles away from town. He and Sampson then happily walked the rest of the way back home.

When he got home, it was just getting daylight, and Cooper was exhausted. Jed met him at the door and could tell that whatever he'd been through was far worse than anything he could've said or done to him, so he just said, "Well, I bet that was fun?"

He laughed, and Cooper chuckled defiantly, "Yeah, it was a blast."

Jed was relieved to have him back home, even if he didn't know what he'd been through during his ordeal. He figured if Cooper wanted him to see, he might tell him all about it when he felt the time was right.

That night, Cooper promised himself that if he ever took off in the desert again, he would make sure he had some water, food, matches, and maybe even a pocketknife.

Later in the evening, the local news that a brave fifteen-year-old Ridgecrest girl held captive for over five years in a shack deep in the desert had escaped her captor. The man that had her was sixty-four-year-old Charles (Charley) Staples. The news said Charles had been arrested twice before and convicted once for child molestation. He'd spent three and half years in prison for that charge before being set free. The news said the girl could get free after all those years and kill her captor and his dog. Ashley didn't want Cooper to get in any trouble, so she told the police she went a little crazy. Not only did she kill Charley, but she killed his dog, too. She said she washed the blood off the knife and cleaned herself before leaving the shack in his pick-up.

The news also talked about how a girl who knew nothing about driving a vehicle took her captor's truck and went back to Ridgecrest. She told the police that once she found her old street, she left the keys in the pick-up and parked them on the side of the road. She then went from house to house until she found her old home. The police never found the pick-up.

After she had reported everything to the police, they went to the old shack where she told them she had been held captive and found Charles Staples' body. They also found the body of the dog lying out in the backyard. They found the chain previously attached to Ashley's wrist inside the house. Everything she had told the police appeared to be true. There was no reason to suspect that anyone else was involved in killing Charley.

***

Chapter 8

On most nights, when Jed got home late, he would drink several beers or do some drugs before bed. It was getting worse for him each day, and it was starting to cost him more than he could afford to pay from his salary at work. Jed had begun to dip into some of the emergency money. To keep from spending all of it, he began to go out at night, break into houses again, and steal things he could sell to make up the extra money he needed for the drugs.

Jed decided it would be an excellent time to talk long with the boys. The boys were about five feet ten inches tall and had long, wavy blond hair down past their ears. They had a muscular build and were a lot heavier than Jed. They were starting to turn into men. He sat them down, "I've been giving it a lot of thought since you told me what you boys did with the dogs and Mr. Pickens. I'm not happy about what you did, but I'm glad you killed him before he killed you boys and your dogs." He looked at Cooper, "Don't ever take off again without letting one of us know where you're going."

Cooper smiled, "Okay, dad, I won't, I promise."

Jed then changed the subject, "I have an idea and want to find out what you boys think about it. Do you remember when I told you my dad, Justin, and I used to steal things into houses?" The boys listened as they shook their heads up and down. "We went all over these three little towns and broke into people's houses at night when they were asleep and stole things. We thought we could sell them fairly easily, and we would store them in that old room behind the house. When we felt like we had a good stash, we'd take everything to Los Angeles and sell it to a guy we called our "Fence."

The people in this area didn't know it was us, but they called the people "Night Crawlers."

Cooper piped up, "That's so cool. I love it."

Jed ignored him and continued, "You boys are almost fifteen years old now, and if you want to learn how to break into houses and steal things, then I'll teach you how we did it without getting caught. You'll have to follow everything I tell you, or we'll all end up getting thrown in jail or killed. I'll work during the day, go out at night, and teach you everything you need to know. No more sneaking out with the dogs and killing animals around here while I'm sleeping. You'll get all the excitement you need from going with me." He looked at Cooper, "Do you understand what I'm saying?" Cooper and Dalton both shook their heads up and down and said they did. "I'll show you what to wear and how to cover your face and hands with charcoal. You'll also learn we don't go out when it rains or snows because someone could follow your tracks back to our house. I'll teach you everything I know to protect each other."

When Jed started talking to the boys, they thought they would be in big trouble for what had happened to Mr. Pickens. They thought he would have their dogs removed, chained up, or worse, brought to the SPCA and put to sleep. He told them he would spend time with them and teach them to break into houses and steal things. They were now in a good mood and no longer afraid of being punished for what they had done. They were thrilled he wasn't going to take their dogs to the pound and have them destroyed.

Jed made it clear that if they were going to work together, they had to change their attitudes and how they talked to him from then on. He told them he wouldn't tolerate disrespect from either of them anymore, and there would be no more lying, regardless of how severe the consequences of telling the truth might be. They both knew what he was saying. They knew they had been getting mouthier with him as they had gotten older. He told them, "There won't be any more cussing around me. To me, that shows a person's stupidity and lack of education. It's also disrespectful to the person you're talking to."

Not wanting to feel any more intimidated and rejected than they had felt the past several days, they immediately agreed to everything Jed wanted them to do. They were excited about breaking into houses where people still lived. They had broken into most empty homes in the area but never where people were still living. They were more than willing to learn the art of stealing.

Cooper said, "Alright. Pretty soon, everyone around here will call us "Night Crawlers." Jed rolled his eyes, "This is going to be a business, Cooper. It's not about trying to become famous. Becoming famous will only get you caught, thrown in jail, or killed."

He slowly began to teach them everything he knew about thieving. As his dad had taught him, he wanted it to become second nature to them, and over the years, Jed had gotten very good at stealing. His every move was easy, just like it had been with his dad. Jed wanted to teach them how to be skilled at stealing as Sherman had been. He wanted them to be completely aware of their surroundings while spying on a house. He told them they had to pay attention to the slightest sound. To find out if everything was okay or if it meant danger for them. He taught them to stay concealed behind the yucca plants and sage bushes. He told them always to have a point where they would wait when they were on the way home from a break-in and ensure nobody had followed them.

Jed told the boys they had to dress in all-black clothing with black "long-johns" underneath them, just like he and Justin used to do. "This high desert always gets cold at night, and I want you to be able to handle the cold weather when we're out there. Our shoes will be black to match our clothes, and we will cover our faces with black charcoal before we're ready to go out on a break-in." His favorite time to go out on the break-ins was around one o'clock in the morning, especially when there was no moon out and windy. Those were the nights and times that Sherman had taught him were best. People and dogs were sleeping, and it was mostly eerie quiet, except for the wind. He told them the night would have to be completely dark to hide their silhouettes, and the wind would help disguise or muffle the noise they made while breaking into the houses. Jed told them they had to hide behind the yucca plants and other desert plants as they crept from place to place. "You must stay very low to the ground as you get up close to the houses. You'll be much harder to see if someone is hiding inside the house and waiting to take a shot at you."

He then told the boys about a couple of close calls he had when he thought the people weren't home, and the homeowners took shots at him and Justin when they tried to break into their house. He laughed and said, "One of those old boys just about got me, but I ducked just in time. The buckshot from his shotgun ripped part of the window frame off right above my head. One almost got Justin one night before he jumped the fence to safety. When you're out there, prepare yourself for anything. You never know what's waiting for you out there. If one of us gets shot and killed, let's try to make sure we take the body back to the house and bury it as we did with my mom, dad, and Justin."

Dalton and Cooper didn't like the sound of that. Dalton said, "That sounds a little creepy!" When Jed said that, everything became severe, and all the joking and kidding stopped. They didn't want anything like that to happen to any of them.

"Good, I have your attention now. It would help if you remembered that Justin and Joshua were killed right out there by people in this town. They'll kill you or me if they catch us trying to steal from them."

Jed took the boys with him off and started taking drives through Red Mountain, Ransburg, and Johannesburg during the day. He wanted them to get familiar with the different houses in the three towns, pointing out the ones he thought would be good targets that didn't have big dogs in the yards. He didn't want them to have any surprises when they started breaking into houses and stealing things.

They went out the first few times, and Jed did mock break-ins to show the boy. They staked out a house for a few days and watched as the people left. Once they were gone, Jed and the boys went up close to the home, and he talked to them about what they needed to do. He had one of them stay back as a lookout while the other went with him as he pretended to break into the house. He would begin their quest to steal things when he felt comfortable with them going with him. It didn't take long because the boys had already developed a criminal attitude long before Jed started working with them. After the first break-in, they could get some nice things to sell, and he complimented them by saying they were natural at it. Their chests puffed out as they accepted what he said with pride.

They continued to break into houses around the Rand area for the following year. They never favored one town; they followed Jed's gut instinct. When they had enough stolen items, they would pack them up and take them to Los Angeles. They always left the dogs at home when they made the trip because there wasn't enough room for them when loaded. The boys loved getting away from the desert and going to Los Angeles. That allowed them to see how the rest of the world lived. They liked Some of it, and some didn't, but it was all new to them, and they liked that.

During one of their trips to Los Angeles, Skeeter and Samson became restless in the enclosed area while the boys and Jed were gone. Samson found a weak spot in the fence and ripped it with his strong jaws and teeth. It took several hours, but he could finally pull the tin back far enough so that he and Skeeter could squeeze through. Once they were out, they went into hunting mode and began looking for something to kill.

It was just getting sundown when they found their first victim. It was a scraggly-looking stray dog that had wandered away from its home, lost and hungry. It looked like it had been without food for a few days and was going from place to place, looking for something to eat. Skeeter and Samson did what they always had done with Cooper and Dalton. They hid behind some bushes as they lay down flat on the ground. Their front feet were out in front of them. They always kept low to the ground just before they were ready to attack something.

Sampson was about ten yards to the side of Skeeter as they waited for the stray to get closer. It had gone to one of the nearby houses and, not finding anything to eat, headed to the next home a few blocks down the road. The dogs sprang into action when he got within about thirty feet of Skeeter. They hit him from two angles and began ripping at him with their powerful jaws. There wasn't anyone there to give them the command to stop, so they tore him to shreds. Once they finished with him, they left his ripped and lifeless body and looked for another victim.

They killed three other dogs in town before they went to the house of Tony Santos. Tony had a large golden lab running free out in the front. Tony wasn't too worried about him because he was a large and tough dog. None of the other dogs in the neighborhood would get too close to him. They tried to stay clear of him when they saw him running around in front of their houses.

When Skeeter and Samson spotted him, he had traveled far away from his house and was about seventy-five yards from his front yard. They quickly got down in a crouched position and started moving toward him. When they were close enough, Skeeter and Samson ran at him hard and attacked him. Samson instantly sunk his jaws into the Lab's neck. Skeeter bit down hard on one of his front legs, and the bone snapped. The Lab tried to fight back as he let out yelping sounds, but Skeeter and Samson didn't loosen their grip on him. It didn't take long, and the dog started limping from Samson's hold on his throat. He had cut off his windpipe, and both dogs began to rip at his throat.

The dogs were so busy attacking the lab that they overlooked Tony, who had heard all the noise from across the road. He came running from his house to the aid of his dog, carrying a rifle with him. He was too late to help his dog, but he saw Skeeter and Samson as they were finishing their attack. Tony took a couple of wild shots at them. The dogs instantly let go of the Lab and started to run. Tony continued to shoot at Skeeter and Samson as they retreated. One of his bullets caught Skeeter in the right side of his back hip, and he went tumbling a few times before getting back up. He could run on three legs and drag his hind leg as they made it a safe distance from Tony's rifle. Once the dogs felt safe, Skeeter sat down and licked at the blood flowing from his wound. After a few minutes, they could make it the rest of the way back home. They squeezed through the opening they had escaped from and back into their yard.

It was late by the time Jed and the boys got home that night, but they first looked for their dogs when they drove in. The dogs were lying next to the door, and Dalton knew something was wrong with Skeeter. He wasn't getting up and acting happy to see them like he usually did when they returned from their trips to Los Angeles. He bent over and patty him on the head. Skeeter tried to stand up, and Dalton saw that his right hind leg was injured. Skeeter couldn't put any weight on his back leg and hip. He let out a yelp when Dalton reached down and tried to touch it. The boys quickly took the dogs into the house to inspect Skeeter. That's when they saw the dried blood all over the dogs. Cooper instantly knew the dogs had gotten out of the fenced-in area, "They got out somewhere and killed some things. Look at all the blood on them. I'll go check the fence." He took a flashlight and started going around the fence until he found where they'd gotten out. He went running back inside to tell Dalton.

Dalton frowned at Cooper, "I think he got shot by someone. There's a hole that looks like a bullet hole that went clean through his hip." The boys looked at each other and wondered how many animals or people the dogs had killed while running free. "Oh, man. I hope they didn't kill someone." He began to bandage up Skeeter's hip, knowing it would take a few months to heal. He bent over and said to Skeeter, "Looks like you're going to have to stay home for a while until that hip heals up, boy." Skeeter gave him a few quick licks in the face.

The next day, the people in Red Mountain found their dead dogs, and Tony told everyone how he shot one of the dogs that had killed him. He said to them that he believed it was some stray wild dogs.

Jed was frustrated that the dogs had gotten out, so he told the boys they'd have to chain them up the next time they went to Los Angeles. When Skeeter was healing, Dalton and Cooper found out Tony Santos had shot Skeeter. They were angry when they found out who shot their dog, and they weren't going to let him get away with it.

Tony had lived in Red Mountain for several years. His parents had emigrated illegally from Mexico when he was a young boy. They lived in Los Angeles while growing up but didn't like the big city. When he married Carmen, they decided to raise their kids in a quiet, small town. Red Mountain was perfect for them, and it reminded him of the little village where he lived in Mexico as a boy. He spoke fluent Spanish and English and worked for a plumbing company in Ridgecrest. All the people in the Rand area knew how good a plumber Tony was, and they called him every time something went wrong with their sinks, toilets, and other plumbing problems.

Now that Tony and Carmen's kids had grown up and moved away, they were just the two living in Red Mountain. Tony was five feet seven inches tall and weighed about a hundred and fifty pounds. He had a distinguished look with a gold tooth in the middle of his upper front teeth. Some people thought it looked a little funny when Tony smiled. He had a passion for fighting game roosters. He had about fifty of them in his backyard in tiny houses resembling A-frame cabins. They had small chains attached to one of their legs where they could only come out of their homes about two to three feet, and that was it. He had set up a watering system so they could have fresh water whenever they wanted.

He worked with his roosters during his days off work. When he thought he had a good fighting rooster, he would take it to Palmdale and enter it in one of the illegal fighting arenas. He would then bet on his rooster to kill the rooster it was fighting. If it were lost, he would discard it in a trash can, like a piece of trash. If it was good enough to win, he was happy and would bring it home and save it from fighting another day.

Dalton and Cooper find out where Tony lives and where he works. They started planning how they would get even for him shooting Skeeter. They waited until Skeeter healed and took him and Samson with them one night to Tony and Carmen's house. They had been watching Tony's house for several days and waited until Carmen had gone to visit one of her kids for the night before they made their move.

They dressed in black clothing and put charcoal on their face and hands as they would break into a house. It was around midnight when they got to the house, and everything was quiet and dark. Tony's truck was parked next to the house, so they knew he was inside sleeping. They had the dogs stay low as they crept slowly up to the house. They tried the locks on the doors and windows, and everything was locked uptight. They went to one of the windows on the other side of the house from where Tony was sleeping and broke a small corner. They waited about twenty minutes to ensure Tony didn't hear it, and Cooper slowly raised the window.

Dalton said he was going inside first because it was his dog that Tony had shot. He slipped through the window and into the house. Dalton approached the back door and let Cooper and the dogs inside. He then tiptoed over to the bedroom where Tony was sleeping. He slowly opened the door and was lying on his back, snoring.

Dalton motioned for Cooper to come over with the dogs. They entered the bedroom and stood close to Tony's bed when Samson sneezed. It instantly woke Tony up when he did that, and he knew he wasn't alone. He was still half asleep when he rose to look around. Dalton had Skeeter grab him by the throat. He told Skeeter to attack but not kill. Skeeter then started ripping at Tony's flesh around his neck and head. He was screaming out in pain, so Cooper had Skeeter stop for a minute while he quickly put a piece of duct tape they had brought over his mouth.

They had brought a nail gun and an extension cord they had stolen. Cooper went over, plugged the line, and attached the nail gun cord. After they let Skeeter rip Tony's body for a few minutes, Dalton stuck the nail gun to Tony's head. Cooper said, "You shouldn't have shot my dog, Tony. Now, you must suffer the consequences of your actions. It looks like you won't be fighting any more roosters." There were five short blasts from the nail gun as Dalton sunk five nails into the side of his head. He then let Skeeter maul Tony for a few minutes to make sure he was dead.

When they finished with Tony, they unplugged the nail gun and the extension cord and took them with them as they left through the back door. On the way home, Dalton said to Skeeter, "That guy shot you. I guess you took care of him, huh, boy?" Skeeter seemed to be happy with himself as he pranced along beside Dalton.

***

Chapter 9

They continued to steal from houses as often as they thought they could get away with it. It wasn't long before some of the old-timers in the area started talking about the "Night Crawlers" being back again. Even though Jed had an excellent job in Ridgecrest, some were even beginning to suspect him and his two sons, who had moved into the Bailey house a few years earlier. They knew the boys had a couple of large dogs in the enclosed property. People rarely saw the boys because they slept during the day and only went out at night.

Jed tried to keep up with the job in Ridgecrest and go out three or four nights a week to scope out a place or break into one with the boys. Things had become very stressful for him. Because of the stress, he began taking more drugs to keep up with everything he was doing. The boys noticed Jed's change and told him he needed to slow down on the drugs. They told him he was beginning to get a little reckless when they went on some break-ins. They told him he wasn't as cautious and meticulous as before. Jed wouldn't listen to them because he couldn't stop the drugs from breaking into houses. He felt he could do nothing to change how things were going in his life. He felt stuck, couldn't quit his job, and couldn't stop doing the drugs.

Then it happened, what the boys feared most. It was just another break-in like so many others they'd been on, but this time, Jed got a little sloppy in his surveillance and didn't wait to see if everyone had left the house. He just assumed that everyone had gone. That was out of character for him because he was always extra careful. Because the people in the Rand area were becoming more aware of the "Night Crawlers," some began setting up decoys to try and catch them. They would pretend they were leaving their houses when someone else pretended to be them while they stayed home. Many began staying home and checking out for someone trying to break in. They were also well prepared with their rifles and pistols to shoot and kill anyone they caught breaking in.

Jed didn't take the time to scope out the house like usual. When he saw the car drive away from home, he thought the owner had left, but it wasn't. It was a decoy that he had to take his place. Assuming the owner was gone, Jed and Cooper slowly approached the house while Dalton kept guard by the fence.

Cooper felt uneasy as he told Jed, "Something doesn't feel right about this, dad. Let's wait a few minutes and check it out a little longer."

Jed was so stressed and anxious that he said, "No, we're ok. Come on, let's get this over with."

Jed broke the window to the room they intended to climb through when they crept up to the house. He usually waited several minutes to see if he heard any noise inside the house, but this time, he seemed to hurry and didn't wait. He was starting to raise the window when two shots from a rifle rang out from inside the house. Both bullets hit Jed, one in the chest and the other in the shoulder. He immediately went down and took a few tumble rolls on the ground. All the while, his instincts told him to retreat from the property. He was bent over and scuffling away as Cooper grabbed him by the arm and started helping him escape as quickly as possible. The man caught a glimpse of them and took two more wild shots at them as they left. Both shots missed his intended target as Jed and the boys took off as fast as possible.

Jed was having difficulty getting back home from the wound to his chest. The boys partly carried him and dragged him to where they always waited to see if anyone had followed them.

When they got there, they sat down for a second, and he said to the boys, "I'm not going to make it, so I want you boys to bury me out in the back of the house."

Dalton cried, "Don't say that, Dad, you'll make it."

Jed could barely whisper, "I love you, boys. Get me back home. I don't want to die out here."

Cooper and Dalton were crying as they carried Jed the rest of the way home.

Just before they got to the gate entrance, Jed's body started limping. Once inside the property, Dalton locked the gate behind them while Cooper carried Jed the rest of the way into his bedroom. Jed had taken his last breath and was gone when he laid him on the bed. Cooper and Dalton were in total shock as they stood there for a few minutes and looked down at their dad. When reality finally set in and they realized he was dead, they screamed in deep pain and began sobbing. They were crying for two reasons: they had just lost their dad and knew they were all alone. From now on, it was only the two of them and their dogs.

The man who shot Jed was fifty-four-year-old Jacob Smallwood, and he lived with his wife, Lisa. They had two grown kids but had moved away several years earlier. After he shot Jed, Lisa immediately called the Sheriff's department and reported what had happened. It took about thirty minutes before the deputies arrived with their lights flashing. A few nearby neighbors had heard the shots and went to Jacob's house with rifles in hand to see what was happening. They were still there with Jacob and Lisa when the deputies arrived.

The deputies asked Jacob what had happened, and he told them everything step by step. The deputies took about forty-five minutes and thoroughly searched the area. They didn't see or find anything or anyone but took a statement from Jacob and Lisa. Jacob told them he swore he shot one of the guys breaking in, but he got away.

After they had been there a few hours, the deputies and neighbors left, and Jacob and Lisa were all alone. It took them another couple of hours to get to bed that night. As they crawled into bed, Jacob loaded the rifle and stood against the nightstand by the bed.

The boys sat on the bed with Jed for a few hours, and Cooper's rage began to build. "I'm going to go get that guy, Dalton. I'm going to kill him for doing this to dad."

Dalton angrily agreed with him in his anger, "That sounds good to me. When do you want to do it."

Cooper said in his haste to get it done, "I'll get the dogs ready to go, and then we'll leave after everyone is gone from his house and that guy is alone and asleep. We'll have Skeeter and Samson rip him apart while I torture him."

They waited until about two in the morning and took Skeeter and Samson to Jacob and Lisa's house. Everyone was gone, and the lights were out. Jacob and Lisa appeared to be asleep for the night. Once in position, they waited and watched everything for several minutes before moving. Everything seemed quiet and normal.

The boys stayed very low and snuck up close to Jacob's house again. Jacob didn't think the thieves would return after he shot one of them. Jacob covered the window with just a sheet. Cooper slowly pulled the sheet off and readied to enter the house.

The boys picked the dogs up one at a time and lifted them through the window. Cooper climbed in after the dogs, and Dalton followed quickly behind. Once inside, they sent the dogs to find the guy they were after. They commanded the dogs to attack, and they immediately ran to the bedroom, looking for their intended target.

It only took a few seconds, and the dogs had Jacob and Lisa pinned down on the bed. Cooper and Dalton then ran into the bedroom, where the dogs had their surprised victims, each by the throat. Cooper had grabbed a long, sharp butcher knife from the kitchen before they left their house and tucked it in his belt. The first thing he did when he entered the bedroom was go after Lisa. She was crying and begging for her life, but Cooper didn't pay any attention to her and quickly took one big swing with the butcher knife and slashed her throat. Blood spurted as he pushed her body to the floor beside the bed.

He went over to Jacob and quickly cut the tendons to Jacob's feet, and he screamed out in pain. Cooper said, "Do I have your attention now?"

Jacob was in terror as he looked up at him and nodded yes.

Cooper growled, "That was our dad you shot and killed earlier tonight. Now we're going to kill you, but I want you to die slowly for what you did to him."

Jacob started crying, and Cooper reached into his mouth with his left hand, grabbed his tongue, and cut it out.

He laughed as he said, "Now try to scream, tough guy."

Dalton didn't care too much for all the torture and slow death thing, "Come on, Cooper, just kill him and get it over with, and let's get out of here before somebody catches us."

By then, Cooper was way past listening to anyone or anything except the crazy person in his head. He tortured Jacob for a few more minutes and then finally took the knife, put it under Jacob's chin, and shoved it as hard as he could up and into his brain. He then cut his throat to make sure he was dead. They had the dogs heal as they left through the back door when they finished. They returned home, stopped at their familiar spot, and ensured nobody had seen or followed them.

When they got home, they continued grieving for the rest of the night as they sat on Jed's bed. Around ten in the morning, Cooper finally told Dalton they needed to make a coffin for their Dad and bury him. Dalton knew he was right and knew it was what their dad wanted them to do. Even so, it was still a hard thing to do. He slowly got up and headed for the back door. Cooper began digging the backyard hole while Dalton made the coffin. They weren't in a hurry to do either, as they took their time getting ready to bury him.

Once Jed was buried and it was over, Cooper sat on the couch with Dalton, "We are all alone, and it's just you, me, and the dogs from now on. We have to take care of each other because nobody else will." They were sixteen years old and felt they could care for themselves.

The next day, neighbors called the Sheriff's Department again, and this time, they reported that they had found the tortured and mutilated bodies of Jacob and Lisa Smallwood. The deputies went out again and spent the entire day investigating the two murders. They put out the word in Red Mountain to look for a guy with several large dogs.

Not taking their time and planning out the murders was a colossal mistake for the boys, and it had now jeopardized their ability to live in Red Mountain. People knew they had big dogs and would have law enforcement check them out concerning the murders.

***

Chapter 10

Things were soon starting to unravel for Cooper and Dalton. When Jed didn't show up for three days, his boss came to his house looking for him. When he arrived, he honked his horn outside the property until Cooper and Dalton couldn't ignore him. Before they went out to talk to him, they made up a lie they would tell him about what happened to their dad. He was frustrated and angry when they first approached his vehicle.

Before they could say anything, he blurted out, "Where the hell is that father of yours? He hasn't shown up for work in three days, and I need him desperately. He didn't even call me to tell me he wasn't coming in and left me in a bad position with my clients."

That's when Dalton spoke, "I'm sorry, Mr. Florio, he won't be coming in. Dad died on Tuesday night."

Mr. Florio's attitude suddenly changed, and he instantly became very apologetic to the boys.

"Oh man, I'm sorry, boys. I had no idea that had happened. I liked your dad."

Dalton said, "Don't worry about it, Mr. Florio. He liked you too and liked working for you."

He then asked them, "What happened to your dad? How did he die?"

Dalton said, "We think it was a heart attack or a drug overdose. We don't know for sure because he died in his sleep."

Mr. Florio seemed shaken when Dalton told him that. He apologized again before he left and went back to Ridgecrest.

They had never had a visit from their Uncle Tucker since they had moved into the place, but they also got a visit from him the next day. It was on a Sunday and his weekend off work. He drove to their front gate and honked his horn until they went out and talked to him. When they got there, he first asked them where Jed was. They tried to tell him the same story they had told Mr. Florio, but he didn't believe what they said. Tucker had already heard the story about Jacob shooting one of the thieves who tried to break into his house. He also listened to the story about how someone had killed the Smallwoods. When they were through telling him their lie, he told them what he'd heard from the people in town.

"Okay, boys, you can tell that story to someone else; I'm not buying it. I just wanted to come by here and let you know that the word around town is that a local guy and his wife died by someone who had a couple of large dogs. It all seems to fit in with you boys and your dad.

The night he died, the local guy told the Sheriff's Deputies that he shot a guy trying to break into his house earlier that night. After the deputies left, he and his wife were tortured and killed in the middle of the night. It sounds like someone was angry and getting revenge against Jacob Smallwood for shooting him or someone he knew." He looked them both in the eyes and said, "Are you still sure you don't know anything about what I'm saying to you? You boys are the only ones around here with huge dogs that are big enough and strong enough to do what they say the animal did to those people."

Cooper frowned, "No, Uncle Tucker, we don't know anything about that."

Tucker ignored what Cooper said and continued to talk and tried to warn them, "The people here in Red Mountain know you boys have those big dogs, and they are starting to think the two murders have something to do with you and your dogs. Some old-timers who knew what happened here years ago with Joshua think it's similar to what happened to him back then. If you boys had anything to do with killing those people, you better think about getting out of town as quickly as possible. The talk around town is that they have formed a vigilante group, and they're coming after you. I don't know, but it might already be too late to get your things together and get out of here. I would leave now if I were you. I hear they're pretty upset and angry about the killings."

Cooper continued lying, "Thanks for warning us, Uncle Tucker, but we didn't have anything to do with killing those people."

Tucker replied, "Okay, well, I just wanted you to know what's going on before they come here and kill you. I don't want to see anything happen to you boys. You're the only family I have left."

Dalton hugged Tucker and thanked him for trying to help them.

As soon as he had left, Dalton had a worried look on his face as he looked Cooper in the eyes, "Okay, Cooper, we better listen to what he's saying and get some of our things and our dogs loaded up and get out of here before it's too late. It sounds like that group of guys are pretty stirred up right now."

Cooper agreed but told Dalton he wasn't sure where they would go.

By then, Dalton was getting a little scared, "It doesn't matter where we go. We have to get out of here before those guys come here and kill us. They won't even listen to anything we try to tell them. You won't be able to talk our way out of this one. You know they'll kill us just like Justin and Joshua did."

Cooper knew Dalton was right, so they grabbed the emergency money, loaded everything in the pick-up, covered it with a tarp, and tied it down. They were ready to leave, but they took a five-gallon can of gasoline and poured it throughout the house before they left. They were going to set it on fire and let it burn to the ground as they left.

Cooper said before they were ready to leave, "If we're leaving, then we're digging dad up and taking him with us. We can't just leave him here."

Dalton replied, "Look, Cooper, we may not have time. They could be here any minute, according to Uncle Tucker."

Cooper said, "I don't care; I'm not leaving here without him."

Dalton didn't like the idea of leaving his dad's body behind any more than Cooper did, but he was trying to be the voice of reason,

"Let's just leave him for now, and we can come back after dark sometime and get him."

While talking about it, they heard a few vehicles pulling up in front of their house. They ran over to the fence to check it out. When they peeked through the holes in the wall, they saw three cars that had pulled up, and five guys with guns got out of them.

When they saw the men get out with guns, they knew they were in trouble, so Cooper quickly ran back into the house and lit it on fire. In an instant, the house became engulfed in flames. Dalton had the two dogs get in the truck cab. Cooper ran back and started the engine while Dalton ran to the gate and quickly opened it. Once he swung it open, he turned and ran around to get in the truck. As he was running back, several shots rang out from the other side of the dirt road.

Dalton was hit twice in the back and fell to the ground. One of the bullets cleared his body as blood spurted from his chest. The other bullet had just grazed the side of his head. He was able to fight his way back up to his feet and stumble over to the open window of the truck. His eyes rolled back into his head as he told Cooper to leave.

With his last few breaths, he yelled, "They've killed me, Cooper, get out of here now. Take care of my dog." Those were the last words he could utter as he stumbled toward the house.

Cooper yelled at him, "No, I can't leave you here, Dalton!"

Cooper started to get out of the truck to go around to help Dalton. He had already staggered over to the door of the house. The flames were shooting out, but Dalton threw himself through the door and into the fire.

Cooper screamed out, "Dalton!" as he watched Dalton burn. Knowing nothing he could do for him, he jumped back in the truck. He knew he had to do what Dalton said and get out of there as quickly as possible, or they would kill him, too.

Instead of risking backing out into the dirt road and getting shot himself, Cooper floored the gas pedal and headed around to the backside of the house. He ran through the fence at full throttle, throwing pieces of it in the air as he returned onto the dirt road and exited Red Mountain. The vigilantes were shooting at his truck as Cooper left. A couple of guys had already headed for their cars to chase after him. He was out of sight when he was on the main road.

Cooper was in a rage. He was hitting the stirring wheel with his fists and sobbing as he raced away at a high rate of speed. Cooper was trying to get out of there before those guys caught up with him. He didn't want them to catch up with him and kill him and the dogs. After going about three miles, I remembered the ravine and Charley Staples pick-up. He turned off the main road and headed down to the secluded canyon where he could hide from everyone.

Once there, he got out of the pick-up, knelt on his knees, and sobbed for several minutes. He stayed in that position long, yelling Dalton's name before Skeeter whined. It suddenly snapped Cooper back to reality, and he was furious at what the vigilantes had done to Dalton. Sitting there and kneeling on the ground, he yelled to the sky, "I'll get you guys for this if it's the last thing I ever do. I promise you that. I'll kill every one of you!" He went over to Charley's pick-up and beat on the hood with his fists a few times. He had never felt that anger and rage; it was almost more than he could stand.

It took several hours for Cooper to calm himself down finally. He just hung out near Charley's pick-up as he cried and thought about how much he would miss Dalton. Cooper felt like Dalton was the only person who knew him. He loved Jed because he was his dad, but he had an extraordinary bond with Dalton. It was almost like they were one. Now that Dalton was gone, Cooper knew he was utterly alone. The only thing he had left was the dogs. It was the emptiest feeling he'd ever experienced in his life.

When it started dark, Cooper was looking at Charley's truck, and he began to wonder what had happened to the old shack where Charley had kept Ashley Stevens captive. He believed it would make him a perfect place to hide from everyone if anyone wasn't living there. Once it got dark, we headed toward Ridgecrest. Once close to town, he could find the minor dirt road leading to the old shack. He got on it and drove until he was about to give up before he spotted the hut.

He put the pick-up lights on a high beam and shined them on the shack. The Sheriff's department had boarded up the front door and windows. Cooper figured they probably did it to keep people from ever using it again. It didn't look like anyone had lived in it since he killed Charley. The little old shack had never had paint on it, and the wood was weathered and brown from years of the hot sun beating down on it. Weeds were growing up around the place.

He exited the truck, grabbed a flashlight, and had the dogs leave. He sent the dogs around to the back of the shack. He wanted to see if they could get a scent of anyone hanging out around the place. Not seeing or hearing anything or anyone, he went to the front door and ripped the boards off. He then sent the dogs in, and they didn't see or hear anyone, so he slowly stepped inside. He thought the place was a little creepy when he first went in. The stain from Charley's blood was still on the floor where he bled out. He told himself that being there always had to be better than sleeping out on the ground somewhere as he looked around. He also figured it would be long before the Sheriff's department would come out again to check on the old place.

For the next few days, Cooper seemed to be in a daze. He was in survival mode, trying to keep his mind off Dalton. He was trying to clean things inside the old dirty shack as he went through every cubby hole. While cleaning, Cooper found a secret hiding place where Charley had hidden some cash in a Mason jar. When he saw it, he quickly reached in and pulled the glass jar out of its hiding place. He unscrewed the lid and poured the money on the kitchen counter. As he counted it out, he found five hundred and twenty-five dollars. He was excited about his new find as he jumped in the air. He still had some money left from his dad's emergency money, but he knew this would also help. He figured with the amount of money he had. It would keep him stocked with food and gas for the truck without worrying about things for a while. He'd brought enough food that it should last him a few weeks.

He dug a large hole in the back and buried all the old bedding and things in Charley. He was lucky that the well had one of those old hand pumps to get enough water for himself and the dogs he needed. He spent an entire day digging a hole and building a makeshift outhouse back to use as a bathroom. He spent another day cutting out a square place in the back of the shack that he would use as a door. He then put the boards back on the front door; that way, if the police came snooping around, they would think it was still empty. He parked the truck around back so he could make a quick get-a-way if he had to.

He was lying on the old beat-up couch next to the dogs on the fourth day. He was relaxing and trying to get his mind off Dalton, his dad, and everything that had happened. Suddenly, an extremely long nine-foot Western diamondback rattlesnake came slithering through the hole in the shack he had cut for a door. It was about fourteen inches in diameter at its circumference, and it had about twelve rattles and a button at the end of its tail. The dogs started growling and sitting up when they first came in. When the snake detected the dogs and Cooper, it curled up in a striking mode by the back door. It raised its upper body about two and a half feet off the floor and looked at Cooper. Its head was about the size of a small football, and when it opened its mouth wide, it showed its long, sharp fangs. They were about two and a half inches long, and he thought they resembled a couple of hypodermic needles. The thought of getting bitten by them sent a cold shiver up Cooper's spine. He figured a bite from that snake could quickly kill him or one of the dogs. As he stared at the snake, he wondered why it sought refuge from the day's heat in the shack instead of hiding in some cool, dark den with other snakes.

He had the dogs stay still as he waited to see if the snake might turn around and return the same way it had come in or if it would make a mad rush toward them. Cooper knew a snake that length would have a long striking distance, and he didn't have anything in the shack that was long enough to keep it away from him and the dogs.

He waited several minutes to see what it would do, but nothing was happening as it curled up. When Cooper or the dogs would make a move, it would raise its head and rattle its tail. It had a distinct sound when it shook its rattles, and there was no mistake. It was a giant rattlesnake. The sound resonated throughout the shack as if echoing off the walls. He finally decided to do something; it didn't look like the monster would leave its newfound home.

He got up slowly, went to the front door, and opened it. He kicked the boards off the front door as he continued to look back at the snake. Once he opened the door and knocked the panels off, he and the dogs could get out without going out the back way and past the snake. He looked outside the shack and found a long metal pipe about ten feet long beside the well. He grabbed the six-foot shovel he had used around the place to clear all the weeds and brush. He went back into the house and began to push and prod the snake with the end of the pipe, just trying to get it to go back the way it came in.

Once he had it outside the door, it turned away from him and started slithering. He took the shovel, ran over, and straddled the snake as it tried to escape. He raised it high in the air and chopped it down on its head with both hands on the shovel. It took two forceful blows before he was able to sever its head. As it squirmed around, dying, Cooper noticed movement inside the snake's body. He then realized why the snake had come into the shack while it was so hot; she would give live birth to her offspring in the hut. Cooper smiled and said, "Man, it's a good thing I killed you. I would've had rattlesnakes all over my place."

He used a few boards he had boarded up the front door as a temporary cover for the back-door hole until he could make a door. He didn't want any other snakes coming in, especially in the middle of the night when they slept. The next time, he and the dogs may not be as lucky as before in getting away from a snake that size.

Cooper checked the house area for snakes and cleaned up the weeds for the next few days. His rage for the vigilantes was building the entire time he worked on it. Cooper couldn't keep his mind off them and what they had done to Dalton. He had to fight the urge to go back to Red Mountain and kill every person in the town.

He was able to calm himself down just enough to try and come up with a plan. Since he had time on his hands, he began to plan out every detail of using the dogs once he found out who the vigilante guys were. He would get them alone and torture them with the dogs before he killed them. He had to find the men's names to find out where they lived. Once he had that information, he could go after them.

***

Chapter 11

Cooper had been thinking about Ashley Stevens since arriving at the old shack. He kept returning to how pretty she was and about the big hugs she gave him the last time he saw her over a year and a half ago. A lot had happened in his life since that time, and his dad and Dalton were dead.

He was starting to run low on dog food, so he decided to go into Ridgecrest and pick up some supplies. While there, he thought he would swing by Ashley's house and see if she still lived there. He went to the pump and got enough water to clean himself up. He brushed his hair and teeth and put charcoal on his scuffed-up black boots. He wore a clean shirt and Levi's to look halfway presentable.

He left the dogs at the shack and went into town. He went straight to the house where he'd dropped Ashley off the last time he saw her. He parked the pick-up and slowly made his way to the door. He was apprehensive because he wasn't sure what kind of reception he might get when she saw him. He knocked a couple of times before Ashley's mom opened the door.

When she did, he said, "Hi, I'm Cooper, and I was looking for Ashley. Is she here?"

Ashley's mom immediately knew who Cooper was because Ashley had told her all about Cooper and how he was the one who found her and set her free. She didn't tell her mom that he was also the one who cut Charley Staples' throat. She smiled and told Cooper to come on in, and she quickly turned and went to Ashley's room to get her.

When Ashley found out Cooper was there, she ran into the living room. When she saw him, she jumped up on him and threw her legs around his waist. Ashley wrapped her arms around his neck hugged and kissed him. She looked different from Cooper. Ashley was no longer the skinny, frail, stringy-haired girl he had seen the last time they were together. She had gained some weight and brushed out her hair. She had make-up on, and he thought she looked beautiful. He was embarrassed at first. He was a little bashful and didn't know how to react to her being so overly friendly.

Ashley took him by the hand with both her hands, led him over to the couch, and sat next to him. Seeing that she was okay alone with him, Ashley's mom left the two of them there and went into the other room.

Ashley smiled at him, "I've tried several times to find you but had no luck. I drove to Red Mountain twice last year to look for you."

Cooper was surprised that she had made all that effort to try and find him. " I didn't know you had done something like that. I'm sorry, we don't know any Red Mountain people, and they don't know us."

Ashley replied, "It's okay, Cooper; I'm so glad you're here now. I've wanted to talk to you and share so much with you."

Cooper was smiling, "Yeah, me too. Thank you for telling the cops that you killed Charley and kept me out of it."

She grabbed his hand, "It was the least I could do after you were so nice to me, setting me free and bringing me back home." She asked Cooper if he would be in town for a few hours and if they could hang out for a while.

He shrugged his shoulder, "Sure, why not? I can do that; I don't have anything else to do. I just came into town for some dog food and groceries. While I was here, I just wanted to check on you."

Ashley went into the kitchen and told her mom they were going down the street to the little park. They were going to hang out and talk for a while. Her mom told her okay but to be careful. She had become slightly overprotective of Ashley since she had her back with the family.

Ashley held Cooper's hand tight as they went to the pick-up and got in. She slid over next to him as they left. Cooper was surprised by the way she had been so compassionate and caring toward him. He never expected her to be that friendly. She treated Cooper like a long-lost boyfriend she hadn't seen for a long time. He had never had anyone treat him like that before in his life. It was a new experience for him, and he liked how she made him feel.

When they got to the park, they sat at one of the tables with bench seats. She slid up close to him and gently kissed him on the cheek. Her lips were warm and soft, sending shivers up his spine when she kissed him. He then reached over and gave her a big kiss on the lips. It was awkward at first because he'd never kissed a girl before.

She giggled like she was embarrassed when he did that.

He said, "What! Did I do it wrong?"

She laughed, "No, silly, it was perfect. I'm just a little shy, that's all."

He then moved away from Ashley and looked her in the eyes. "Hey, Ashley, there are some things you don't know about me before you get too friendly with me. We need to talk to tell you what's been going on with me since I saw you last. He figured he might as well get things out in the open if she wanted to tell him never to come by and see her again. "You may not like me once I tell you these things."

She smiled and leaned back, "Okay, Cooper, I'm all ears; you can tell me anything you want."

He didn't know where to start and slowly told her he had a couple of large dogs that he and Dalton had trained, and now they were with him. He told her that the dogs would kill anything he wanted them to, including people. "You know, you already met Samson. He was with me when I first saw you at the shack." He thought that would be enough to scare her away, but she smiled and just sat and listened. He then told her how he, Dalton, and his dad would go out at night and break into houses in the three little towns around Red Mountain and steal things. Once they had enough stuff, they would sell it to Los Angeles.

He said some old-timers around that area called them "Night Crawlers." He told her that his dad got careless one night and killed a guy in Red Mountain. "I killed the guy that did it, along with his wife." She wasn't deterred by what he was saying as she seemed fascinated with everything he told her.

He then told her about his twin brother Dalton and how they had a secret dialog, and he even knew what the other one was sometimes thinking. He told her about the vigilante group formed in Red Mountain and how they came after him and Dalton and killed Dalton in the process. He said to her that he didn't have any other place to go and had been hiding out at the old shack where Charley had held her prisoner, and he'd been there a few weeks since Dalton died.

She then gasped, "That old place? I can't believe you're there. I hate that place."

Cooper said, "I know you do, Ashley, but I couldn't think of any other place to go hideout for a while. I've removed everything that belonged to Charley and cleaned the place up. I also have to tell you that when I find out who the guys are in the vigilante group, I'm going after them, and I'm going to kill every one of them. I have to find out their names and where they live."

It surprised Cooper when Ashley said, "I'll help you find out who they are if you want me to and what each of their weaknesses is."

He jerked his head back, "I don't want you to get involved with anything like that. I don't want you to get in trouble just because of me."

She spoke softly, "You don't understand Cooper. What that older man Charley did to me screwed my head up well. I've been going to the psychiatrist for help since you brought me home. The therapist told me I have what they call rape trauma syndrome. I was angry, degraded, frightened, and confused when it first happened. Since returning home, I've withdrawn from my family because I was ashamed and embarrassed about what he did to me. Charley had destroyed my self-esteem and my dignity. He took away all my self-worth, and I've had difficulty thinking that someone would ever want me or love me. I have difficulty returning to school because I can't concentrate on schoolwork. The state paid my mom to hire a tutor, so I got homeschooled instead of attending a regular school. I can't and don't want to be around any of those kids from school. Now I have an anger problem, and I want to hurt people that do bad things to other people. I can't help myself; it's how I feel inside. I'm not like some of those girls that get abducted. I can't just forget what happened to them and go on with their lives—helping you might be an excellent way to eliminate some of my pent-up anger and frustration. I haven't been able to date any guys or have an everyday life since I got home.

I've spent much time thinking about you since I first met you, and you set me free." She leaned in and kissed him again. Cooper loved the attention as they talked and occasionally kissed for a few more hours before he said he had to get going. Cooper told her he needed to get back to his dogs. He had left them in the shack and knew they had to be out soon to go to the bathroom.

While driving her back to her house, he told her that if she wanted to help him find the names of the vigilante guys, then he'd pick her up on Monday morning before noon. They would then go to Red Mountain and see if they could find out what he desperately wanted to know.

Before she left the pick-up, she gave Cooper a big kiss and a hug and told him she would see him on Monday. "I'm so glad you came back to check on me, Cooper."

He smiled at her, "Yeah, me too, Ashley."

After he dropped her off, Cooper thought about how Ashley had reacted to everything he told her about himself and what he would do to the vigilante guys. She wasn't fazed by what he told her. She understood his anger and could relate and sympathize with him. Cooper knew she was angry about what Charley had done to her. He felt like she probably would've helped him hunt the guys down and kill a couple of them herself if he would let her. He knew he didn't want her to do that because he wanted to do it himself.

Cooper went to the market, got what he needed, and returned to the shack. They were excited to see him when he returned to the dogs. After they were relieved, they returned in, and Cooper dished them up some much-needed dog food. He sat on the couch, and his mind was deep in thought as the dogs gobbled down their food.

He thought about his day with Ashley, but his mind kept going back to the guys who killed Dalton. Sitting there, he fanaticized what Cooper would do to each of them when he found out who they were. He formulated a plan of how he would kill each of them. Cooper wanted to take his time and not get in a big hurry. The last time he made a hasty decision, it got Dalton killed. He didn't care if killing them took him a year or more; he just wanted to torture them with the dogs before they died.

The following Monday, he left the dogs in the shack and headed to Ashley's house. When he got there, she gave him a warm welcome she had a few days earlier. As they drove to Red Mountain, he found that she was easy to talk to, and he liked that about her. They had a weird but strong connection with each other.

Before he got to Red Mountain, he told her he had to change vehicles with Charley's old truck. He told Ashley that the last time he was driving his dad's truck, the vigilantes were shooting at it as he headed out of Red Mountain. He told her he couldn't very quickly drive it into town. When Cooper got to where he'd hidden the truck, he pulled off the road and entered the secluded ravine. Everything was as when he left.

When they got in Charley's truck, the battery was dead and wouldn't start because parking it there had been a while since. He used his jumper cables to start it and air the tires with a hand pump. As they headed into Randsburg, Cooper said, "I thought that maybe I could take you to "The Joint" in Randsburg, and you could order some lunch. While eating, you could ask the waitress who the vigilante guys who took the law into their own hands might be.

She smiled at Cooper, "Not a problem, I'll play it real cool, and if the waitress knows them, I'll find out who they are."

Cooper smiled back at her, "I know you will, Ashley.

I know you can get the information I need." He was playing on her ego just a little, but he was good at doing that and manipulating people.

When they got to Randsburg, Cooper dropped Ashley off near the bar, drove down the street a few blocks, and parked in a non-conspicuous place while he waited. When she went into the Joint, she was smiling and bubbly. Ashley instantly hit it off with the people working there. She told them she was visiting from out of town and heard it was an excellent place to get a burger and fries.

The waitress was an older woman about her mom's age, so they instantly felt comfortable with each other. She ordered the special: a cheeseburger, fries, and a coke. While waiting for it to come, she talked to the waitress about how dead the little towns were. They talked for a while before she said, "My friend that lives in Red Mountain was telling me about a bunch of guys that went after a couple of brothers, and they shot and killed one of them not too long ago. That sounds pretty exciting."

The waitress said, "Yeah, the boys supposedly killed a guy and his wife in Red Mountain, so the neighbors got a group of men together and went after them. I heard they shot one of them, and then he ran into his house they had set on fire and burned himself up. The other one got away."

Ashley said, "Man, that takes a lot of nerve for those guys to go after a couple of mean killers like that." She had done an excellent job setting the waitress up, "Does anyone know who the vigilante guys were?"

The waitress paused to think, "I heard two of them were Jim Larson and his son Kerry, but I don't know about the others. I think Jim and Kerry are the ones that were going around town bragging about shooting the boy before he threw himself into the fire."

Ashley said, "That sounds so gruesome. What a terrible way to die."

The waitress wrinkled up her face, "It does, doesn't it?"

They talked a while longer about everyday things, and then Ashley finished her food, thanked the waitress as she paid for it, and left.

She then walked down the street to where Cooper was anxiously waiting to hear what she had to say. He was overly nervous from anticipation. When she jumped in the truck, she had a big smile: "I got the names of two of them. That's all the waitress knew. I'm sorry, Cooper, she didn't know the other three men."

He said, "That's alright, Ashley, that's all I need. I'll get the names of the rest once I meet face-to-face with one of those two guys."

She told him their names and said they were father and son. She told him they were going around town bragging about shooting Dalton before he threw himself in the fire. When she said that, the rage welled up in Cooper once again, and he felt the blood rush to his face. He had to fight to control his anger. "Those pieces of crap had to shoot an unarmed person in the back because they're nothing but a bunch of cowards. They won't be bragging about it for long." He then returned to the ravine, traded trucks, and returned to Ridgecrest.

He thanked Ashley a few times on the way back and told her he would keep in touch with her over the next few months and let her know how things were going. He kissed her, dropped her off at her house, and returned to the shack.

***

Chapter 12

He waited until Friday, and it was the middle of the afternoon when Cooper loaded up Skeeter and Samson and headed to Red Mountain. When he got there, he used his charm when he stopped a woman walking her dog and asked her if she knew where the Larson lived. Feeling comfortable with him, she gladly told him where they lived and even gave him directions on how to get there. Once he knew where they lived, he returned to the ravine and parked his truck, waiting for darkness to fall.

He used the same technique when he broke into the houses. He wore all black and painted his face with charcoal. When it was dark, he took the dogs, and they hiked the three miles back to Red Mountain, very close to the Larson house. Kerry's pick-up, another older pick-up, and a car were in the driveway. Cooper could tell it was a younger person's truck because it looked like a four-wheeler. It was raised off the ground about two feet and had all the bells and whistles. He had the dogs lie down and relax as he watched to see if he could get a good look at Kerry if he came out of the house.

He waited a few hours before Kerry went out for the evening. Cooper chuckled, "Look at that chubby belly on that big slob. He either loves his mom's cooking or drinks too much beer." He figured Kerry had to be in his mid-thirties. After he got in his truck and left, Cooper said, "I got you, sucker. It's just a matter of time, now." He then hiked back to where his pick-up was hidden and cleaned the charcoal off his face before heading back to the little shack.

The next day, after he got up, he took the dogs and started looking through the desert for wood. He carried bundle after bundle and threw it in the back of the pick-up. He continued to do that for the next few days until he had a pile of wood about five-foot-high and about ten feet wide. He stacked it out behind the shack, about twenty yards from where he parked his truck.

After the weekend, he figured if Kerry had a job, he would get up early each morning and work. He drove back to Red Mountain just before daylight. Cooper had the dogs with him and hid by the old Silver Dollar Saloon. He waited there to see if Kerry would leave Red Mountain. He figured that if Kerry had a job, he had to pass right by to get to where he was going.

He figured right, and it was about seven-thirty in the morning when Kerry came tearing past him in a big hurry like he was late for work. He pealed rubber as he turned north onto Highway 395. Cooper slowly pulled in behind him and kept a safe distance between them. When he got to the turnoff east to Ridgecrest, Kerry went west into Inyokern's tiny town. After a few minutes, Kerry entered a quick-stop store and came out with what Cooper believed was a cup of coffee. He then got back onto the road that went into Ridgecrest. You could see cars coming and going for miles in either direction. Cooper followed him to where he worked, and once he was satisfied, he turned around and left. He knew his plan for Kerry was now in place. He knew he could get him either while working or on his way home.

Cooper got up early the next day and followed Kerry without the dogs. He didn't want to have any distractions when he grabbed Kerry. On this morning, when Kerry went in to get coffee at the little store, Cooper jumped out of his pick-up, went over, and nailed a significant spike in Kerry's right-front tire while still inside. The air was slowly hissing out as Kerry entered the truck and quickly headed toward Ridgecrest. He was so hurried that he didn't notice the tire was starting to go flat. He had gotten about three miles when he pulled off to the side of the road with the flat tire. Cooper waited until there wasn't any traffic coming or going for several miles in either direction or pulled in behind Kerry's truck.

When he exited his truck, Cooper smiled and was friendly as he asked Kerry if he needed help.

Kerry was pissed off and not in a good mood to be bothered by anyone now. He said in an angry voice, "No, I can handle it myself."

Cooper replied, "I'd be glad to help if you need a hand?" Kerry didn't say anything as he started trying to figure out how he would change the tire. He had already removed the tire and had his jack out when Cooper went up next to him and stood there trying to talk to him.

Cooper waited a minute or so for him to bend down and try to loosen one of the nuts holding the tire. Cooper pulled a hammer from the back of his pants and hit Kerry in the head. He didn't hit him hard enough to kill him, just enough to knock him out. Kerry went down instantly, and Cooper quickly grabbed him by the neck of his shirt and dragged him to the back of his truck. He let down the tailgate and lifted him onto it and into the vehicle's bed. Quickly duct-taping his mouth and eyes. He put Kerry's hands behind his back and wrapped them and his feet with duct tape several times. He then hog-tied him (his feet to his hands) so he couldn't move once he woke up. After he was loaded up, Cooper headed back down towards Ridgecrest and the minor dirt road that led to the shack.

When Kerry woke up, they were already traveling on the dirt road. He was being thrown from one side of the truck's bed to the other as Cooper took the narrow turns faster than average to screw with him. He laughed as he purposely took a few of them too sharp and too quickly to throw him across the bed and hit the other side.

Once back at the shack, Cooper went and let the dogs out. He told them to sit as he dragged Kerry out by his feet and let him hit the ground. Cooper cut the duct tape from his feet so Kerry could walk. He picked Kerry up by the collar and led him into the shack. Cooper sat him down in a chair and then put duct tape around his feet again. He also wrapped duct tape around his chest and the chair so he couldn't stand up.

He then ripped the duct tape from Kerry's eyes.

It took a few seconds for him to focus on Cooper, but when he did, Cooper asked, "Hey, fat ass, do I look familiar to you?"

Kerry shook his head no.

Cooper snarled, "Take another closer look. Don't I look a little like the unarmed young guy you shot in the back at Red Mountain?"

Kerry's eyes then got wide with fear as he just sat there.

Cooper raged, "That young guy you shot in the back was my twin brother, and you will die for killing him. You and your little group of vigilante's friends are all going to die for taking the law into your own hands." He then took the duct tape off Kerry's mouth, "I want to know the names of the other three men besides your dad who were part of your little group. If you don't tell me, I'll let Skeeter and Samson here have some fun chewing on your body as they rip it apart."

He was stammering like he didn't know who they were, so Cooper gave Skeeter and Sampson the command to attack but not kill. They knocked Kerry and the chair over and began ripping at his flesh. Cooper let them tear at his flesh for about thirty seconds before he had them heal and sit next to him.

Then he went over and propped Kerry back up, and he said again while blood flowed from his fresh wounds. "You need to tell me who the other three guys are that you and your dad were with, Kerry. If you don't tell me, I will keep turning the dogs loose on you until you do. You can make it hard on yourself, or you can make it easy. It's all up to you."

Kerry started to say he didn't know again when Cooper interrupted him and said, "That sounds like it's going to be the wrong answer, Kerry. Are you sure you don't want to change your mind and tell me who they are before I turn my dogs loose on you again?"

Kerry sat there for a minute, then blared out their names. "The other three guys are Ted Summers, Mark Silvers, and Frank Townsend. They're all friends of my dad."

Cooper said, "Thank you, Kerry. Now, don't you feel much better than you have that off your chest?" He wasn't expecting an answer as he took some more duct tape and put it across Kerry's mouth. He was excited that he had the names of the other three guys.

He then went to the kitchen, got a butcher knife, and returned to Kerry. He lifted his right hand and said, "Is that the finger you used to pull the trigger of the gun you shot my brother with?" Not getting an answer, he pulled Kerry's right index finger out straight and cut it off. He threw it on the counter and said, "Don't think you'll need that anymore, Kerry."

He tortured Kerry again the next day as he turned the dogs loose on him twice and let them rip at his body. It was about two in the afternoon when he left Kerry sitting in the chair with the dogs watching him. He went outside and started the fire of the wood he'd stacked up outback. He waited about ten minutes until the flames shot up in the air several feet and then went back inside. He put a thick rope around Kerry's body, just under his armpits. He cut the duct tape around his legs and walked him out by the fire.

On the way there, he laughed, "We're going to have a Weenie roast, Kerry, and I want you to be part of it." When Kerry stood right in front of the fire, he taped his legs again with duct tape. He waited just a minute, then said, "I just want you to see and feel what my brother Dalton saw and went through just before he died." He then ripped the duct tape from Kerry's eyes and shoved him headfirst into the vast fire. He waited until he had been in the fire for several minutes and had quit squirming around, and then he pulled his charred body from the flames. By then, the rope had caught on fire, and he had to put it out. He wrapped Kerry's body in a blanket, took him to the back of his pick-up, and threw him in the truck's bed.

He left his body in the truck until it was almost midnight. Then he loaded the dogs and said, "Come on, boys, we have a delivery to make." He headed back to Red Mountain, and when he got to the front of the Larson house, it was about two in the morning, and everyone was asleep. He pulled up out in front, quickly pulled the charred body out, and dumped it in the dirt road in front of the house. He was there in less than ten seconds, then quickly sped away.

He knew Jim Larson and his wife would be devastated when they found out their son was dead. He'd already decided that he wouldn't kill Jim immediately. He wanted him to suffer for a while as he thought about how his son had died such a horrific death.

***

Chapter 13

The following day, Cooper got up early and threw dirt over the ashes from the massive fire he'd built. He didn't want anyone coming upon the shack and thinking someone was living in and around it. Cooper decided to take a few weeks and let the shock of Kerry Larson's death die down a little in Red Mountain. He had the other three men's names, so he didn't have to get in a big hurry to kill them. He knew they would be there when he was ready to go after them.

During that time, he decided to spend some time with Ashley. A few days after he killed Kerry, he cleaned up and went to Ridgecrest. When he got there, Ashley was very excited to see him.

When they were alone, she pulled him aside and whispered, "Oh, my gosh, Cooper." I saw it on the news about Kerry Larson. Everyone in Red Mountain and the Rand area is upset about his death."

Cooper said, "Yeah, well, he deserved everything he got. It wasn't any worse than what he did to Dalton. Nobody made a big deal about it when Dalton died from the vigilante group."

He told her he had found the names of the other three men in the vigilante group. He said that Kerry gave them to him before he killed him. He told her he needed her to find out everything she could about them, where they lived, worked, and what they did in their spare time.

He gave her the names, and Ashley said, "That's not a problem. I'll go to the computer and get some information about them from there. I'll drive to Randsburg and talk to the waitress again if necessary. She'll give me everything she knows."

Cooper thanked her, and after he relaxed, they began enjoying their time together.

They had developed a good bond, and we treated each other like boyfriend and girlfriend. Cooper never pushed Ashley to do anything she didn't want to do. He always showed her total respect. Cooper didn't ask questions about what had happened to her when she was with Charley. He knew that was part of her life; she wanted to try and forget. It didn't make him feel any different about her; she was beautiful to him, and that's all that mattered.

For the next few weeks, Cooper would leave the dogs at the shack while he went into town and visited with Ashley. They went to the movies together and had lunch at a few local fast-food restaurants. Their kissing became make-out sessions, and soon, they were in a full-fledged relationship. The empty feeling of missing Dalton was temporarily forgotten into the semblance of happiness while he was with her.

Ashley was finally starting to feel good about herself again. She realized someone could care about her for who she was, not how she thought of herself. It was good for them, as twisted as their relationship might have been. They felt like they had each other to lean on. At the end of the second week spent with Ashley, she discovered what he needed to know about the three men on his list. Cooper just listened as she read what she had written on a tablet.

"I found out that Jim Larson was the guy that was pushing everyone to go to your house that day and kill you and Dalton. He's fifty-eight years old, and his wife's name is Janelle. His hair is short, and he has a stocky build for his five-foot-ten-inch frame. He's retired and doesn't do much but piddle around his property. He got everyone to join the group when he told them he'd been around when Joshua Bailey killed the three men in Red Mountain. He told the men that Joshua lived in the same house and had a large killer dog like Cooper and Dalton. He believed there was a connection and that the boys had killed Jacob and Lisa Smallwood. He got everyone fired up to go to your house that day."

"One of the other guys in the vigilante group was forty-eight years old Frank Townsend. He lives in a small house in Johannesburg. His wife died five years ago from cancer, and his kids moved away. He works at the China Lake Military Base in Ridgecrest. He's five feet nine inches tall, keeps his head shaved, and wears a baseball cap everywhere.

The trouble is he doesn't go to very many places. He watches television at night once he gets home from work. He's deathly afraid of all snakes, especially rattlesnakes. He has a pretty boring life. He was best friends with Jacob and Lisa Smallwood and was looking for revenge for his best friend and wife's death."

"Ted Summers is married and has two kids living at home. They are both girls, and they go to the local high school. He controls every aspect of his wife Judy and his two daughter's lives. He seems to be a control freak. He works as a supervisor at Ridgecrest for a construction company. He's overconfident and drives around in his company pick-up all day, spouting orders to people. He also wears a baseball cap most of the time. He's fifty-two years old and six-foot-one-inch tall. He spends many days off in the desert riding his dirt bikes."

"Mark Silvers is just plain weird. He doesn't work and lives off disability, and he can get paid under the table for his little work. He has a drinking problem at times and has gotten a few D.U.I.. over the years. He's been married and divorced several times and is not living with anyone. He's five foot eleven inches tall and skinny. He has a couple of big dogs and lots of guns and ammunition. He calls himself a Patriot and has told people he'll be ready when the Muslims or the Communists try to take over America. He joined the vigilante group because he had nothing to do and felt it was for a good cause."

Cooper thanked Ashley for her help, "When I get through with these guys, they'll wish they stayed home that day instead of joining that stupid group." Before he left, he told her he would be busy for a few weeks and not to get upset if she didn't see him for a while. He left and went back to the shack. When he arrived, he sat on the couch and thought about the four men he would go after. He decided his next target was going to be Ted Summers.

A few days later, Cooper found out where Ted Summers' office was in Ridgecrest and applied for a job. He asked if it was easy working for Ted. She rolled her eyes and said, "The guys sometimes say it is good, and other times he's a hard nose, and you can't please him." He asked if it would be possible to come in on Saturday and talk to Ted about a job in person instead of handing him an application. She looked at Ted's schedule and told him he was off Saturday and Sunday, so it would have to be the following week. After hearing that news, he told her he would return next week and thanked her for her help.

On Friday night, Cooper decided he would camp out at the place where he'd parked Charley's truck until he met up with Ted. He packed up the dogs and headed to Red Mountain. Cooper switched trucks just before dark and drove by Ted's house. He had a couple of his dirt bikes strapped down in the bed of his vehicle, ready to go early the following day.

Once Cooper knew he was going out into the desert the next day, he returned to his campsite and waited until almost daylight. He didn't sleep that night as he sat up and thought about Dalton and how he would get revenge on Ted Summers.

When it was time to go, he threw some ropes in the bed of the old truck, went to a spot, and parked where he could watch for Ted's truck as he left. Ted was up early and left at the first light of day. Cooper pulled out not too far behind him and followed him.

He kept a close eye on Ted's vehicle as he turned off a dirt road and headed deep into the desert. It took about thirty minutes for Ted to get to where he was going before he parked and got out. He quickly started taking the chains and locks off one of the dirt bikes and unloaded it.

Cooper had parked a long distance away and could barely see Ted's figure as he unloaded one of the bikes. He was so busy with what he was doing that he hadn't noticed Cooper had followed him to his favorite hiding place.

When Ted rode off on one of his bikes in the distance, Cooper took the dogs, grabbed the gas can from the back, and the duct tape. He put a rope around his shoulder and hiked ahead to where Ted parked his truck. He broke the window, opened the door, and had the dogs pile in the cab. He brought extra water and food for himself and the dogs as if he would be there all day. A whole five-gallon can of gas was sitting on the passenger side of the pick-up. That's when Cooper knew Ted would return to fill his tank or possibly get on the other bike in a few hours.

They waited in the truck until about ten o'clock when they saw a dirt bike approaching. Cooper had the dogs jump out of the vehicle, and they all found a place to hide in the sagebrush not too far away. Cooper said to the dogs, "Get ready, boys. Here he comes." The dogs were anxious as they lay down like they always did before they went on an attack.

When Ted approached the pick-up, he parked the bike next to it and took off his helmet. He then noticed the broken window of his truck. Ted immediately began cursing and kicking the dirt in anger. He started looking in all different directions for the person that had done that to his truck.

Cooper waited until he thought Ted was the most vulnerable. He then gave the dogs the command to attack but not kill. They blindsided Ted and knocked him to the ground. He immediately started trying to pull the pistol with which he had tucked his pants to kill snakes, but it was too late. Samson had him by the throat, and Skeeter had him by the arm in a matter of seconds. Once the dogs had him under control, Cooper calmly walked over, picked up a hand-sized rock, and hit Ted across the head with it. Not enough to kill him, but just enough to stun him and calm him down.

He was lying on his back, so Cooper flipped him over on his stomach and then wrapped the duct tape around his hands a few times so he couldn't get loose. He also taped his feet together and put a couple of tape strips over his eyes and mouth. Once he had Ted where he wanted him, he took his time and started doing everything very organized.

He tied a rope around Ted's shoulders and then tied it firmly to the back of the dirt bike. He put gas in the cycle from the can before he started it up. When Ted firmly attached the rope to the bike, he got on the dirt bike and started dragging him through the desert behind the bike. He sped up to about thirty miles per hour, and Ted's body was flipping from one side to the other as he bounced off the sage bushes and rocks. Cooper made a few figure eights and drove across anything that looked like it would beat Ted's body up. He did that for about ten minutes before he pulled his dirty, limp body back to the pick-up.

Ted's broken body wasn't trying to fight it anymore, but he was still alive. Cooper then got behind Ted's back, lifted him up and into the truck, and put him in the driver's seat. He tied his hands to the steering wheel so he couldn't jump out. Cooper poured the rest of the five-gallon can of gas on Ted and in the truck's cab and threw some of it on the outside of it. He loosened the rope from the bike, lifted it, and threw it in the truck's bed with the other one.

While preparing everything, he went over to Ted and ripped the duct tape from his eyes. "I want you to know that the young guy you and your vigilante friends killed was my twin brother. He didn't have any weapons on him when you guys shot him in the back." Ted opened his eyes for a second when Cooper told him that.

He untied the rope from Ted's body, rolled it up, and put it around his shoulders. He had the dogs get back as he lit the gasoline on fire, and the truck instantly went up in flames. He threw the five-gallon empty can into the bed of the vehicle. He took his gas can with him as he and the dogs quickly headed back to his pick-up.

There were a few explosions from the gas tanks and the five-gallon can as they returned. He quickly returned to the main road when they got to the truck. Once on the main road, he then headed north to the ravine. On the way back, he said aloud, "That's two of those pieces of crap, Dalton, just three more to go."

He returned to the ravine, changed vehicles, and then headed north on 395 toward the shack. He passed a few police vehicles and a fire truck going in the opposite direction. He figured they were going to the crime scene where he'd killed Ted Summer.

***

Chapter 14

Cooper returned to the Shack and tried to relax for a few days. One afternoon, he was sitting with the dogs when he heard a vehicle approaching the shack from the distance. Cooper quickly got the dogs outside and closed the back door behind them. He had the dogs jump in the pick-up cab and left the driver-side door open for them, just in case he had to use them to attack someone. He took a tin cup in the truck, walked over to the well, and pretended he was getting water from it. As the vehicle approached, Cooper soon could tell it was a Sheriff's Department truck. He said, "Okay, Cooper takes a deep breath and plays it cool."

A deputy named Richard Gilbert had driven up and parked his vehicle not too far from where Cooper was standing. He had his hand over the holster of his gun when he first got out of his truck.

Once he saw Cooper as a young man in his teens, he relaxed slightly. The first question he asked Cooper was, "What are you doing way out here in the desert?"

Cooper calmly replied, "I just brought my dogs out to run, sir. They've been cooped up in my backyard for a couple of weeks now, and they love it out here in the desert."

He pointed back at the dogs sitting in the pick-up. They were watching very intently as Cooper talked to the deputy. They were ready to spring into action if Cooper commanded them to attack.

"They got thirsty, and I found this old well the last time I was out here, so I was just getting ready to pump them some water."

Deputy Gilbert looked over at the shack and could tell it still had some boards across the front door and windows. It didn't look like anyone was living in the place to him. He said, "Have you seen anyone around here that looks like they might be just hanging out?"

Cooper said, "No, I haven't seen anyone out this way, just the dogs and me. That's why I bring them out here to get away from everyone.

Plus, I can get them fresh water after they run for a while. That old run-down place looks like nobody's lived there for some time."

He then asked Deputy Gilbert what he was doing in the desert far from town.

He said, "We had some problems a few days ago with a few local guys killed out in the desert. One was near the desert of Red Mountain, and the other was dumped back at his house in Red Mountain."

Cooper had to turn his head away toward the well and refrain from smiling as he asked, "So what happened to the guys?"

He replied, "Some "Sicko" taped one guy to the steering wheel of his truck, poured gasoline all over him and it, and then lit it on fire. Burned the poor guy to a crisp." He also burned the other one, but he did it someplace else and then dumped him back home.

Cooper replied, "That sucks. Who would do something like that?"

The deputy said, "I don't know, but you need to keep an eye out while you're out in the desert. That guy is still out there someplace."

Cooper said, "Okay, I will contact the deputy, but I think me and the dogs are just about done for the day. We'll head back to Ridgecrest when I get them some water."

Deputy Gilbert said, "May not be a bad idea. You don't want to be out this far, especially after dark, with that nut case running loose."

Deputy Gilbert then decided he would get a closer look at the shack as he walked toward it.

He looked around the front and side of it when Cooper yelled, "Hey, deputy, you should try some of his cold water before you head back to town. It's freezing."

Deputy Gilbert couldn't resist, "That's not a bad idea." He turned around and walked over to Cooper as he pumped some water. He handed the deputy a tin cup of fresh cold water, "Try this. It's pretty good stuff."

He gulped and said, "Well, guess I should be heading back. Keep your eyes open while you're out here."

Cooper said, "Thank you for letting me know, Deputy; I'll be extra careful."

Cooper began pumping more water as deputy Gilbert returned to his truck. Cooper watched over his shoulder as he turned his vehicle around and headed out of the dirt road where he entered.

Once his truck was out of sight, Cooper laughed aloud and said, "Nut case, huh, that's funny." He repeated the words "Sicko" a few times and laughed aloud each time he said it. "If I'm such a "nut case" and a "sicko," then why don't all those smart guys from law enforcement know who I am? Why can't they figure it out?" At that point, he was feeling invincible and proud of himself.

A few days later, his compulsion to go after the other men started to eat at him again. He decided he was going to go after Mark Silvers next. He lived across the dirt road and down just a little way from Cooper's number one enemy, Jim Larson. He knew he had to plan things out very carefully because Mark had dogs. Cooper also had tons of weapons, so he could quickly kill him if he made a mistake. Especially if he knew he was the next one on Cooper's list to kill.

The next day, Cooper drove into Ridgecrest, went to the Wal-Mart store, and purchased a stun gun. It was strong enough to knock a man down. He then moved back to the ravine and traded vehicles. He had the dogs get down low in the seat as he slowly drove by Mark Silvers' house. He saw Mark drive a green four-wheel-drive older model jeep parked next to the house. He carried a locked toolbox in the back of it. A couple of large dogs ran toward his truck, barking when Cooper passed. He saw Mark in the yard, and they waved to each other as he passed by.

Cooper camped in the ravine with the dogs for a couple of days while he just watched to see what Mark was doing each day. He got up early, hiked up close to his house, and was protected from a hidden location as Mark came and went several times during the two days.

Mark always left and came back the same way each time. After watching him, Cooper devised a plan and knew what he wanted to do.

Not wanting to meet Mark on his turf, Cooper got up early for fear of being shot, drove Charley's pick-up, and parked it near the end of Mark's road. He sat there for about three hours looking through his rear-view mirror before he saw Mark's jeep coming from his house and heading toward him. Cooper quickly jumped out of the pick-up and raised his hood. He told the dogs to get down on the floorboard, and they immediately responded.

When Mark got close to him, he stepped out in the middle of the dirt road and started waving his arms for help.

Mark pulled beside him and said, "What seems to be the problem here, sonny?"

Cooper replied, "I think it's my battery, Sir. It must have died on me. I had trouble with it this morning before I left home. Do you have any jumper cables with you?"

Mark said, "Yeah, I have some in my toolbox. I'll grab them. We'll try that and see if it will get you started again."

He seemed like a pretty nice guy to Cooper and very helpful. He was in his mid-forties with light brown hair and a friendly smile. He had one of those old straw cowboy hats where the brim was bent down in the front, and he was wearing cowboy boots. He could tell he'd had that hat for a while from the looks of it.

As Mark got the cables, Cooper grabbed the stun gun and stuck it in the back of his pants. Mark pulled his jeep up next to the truck, and just as he was hooking up the cables, Cooper looked around to make sure nobody was watching as he shot him with the stun gun and a few million volts of electricity. He went down and started kicking like he was having convulsions. Cooper quickly flipped him onto his stomach. He then put his hands behind his back and duct-taped a strip on his mouth and feet. Then, he lifted him and threw him in the truck bed. When he had him lying face down, he quickly hog-tied his hands to his feet with the tape so he couldn't move. After loading Mark up, he took off, leaving his jeep in the middle of the road. He had picked up Mark's old hat and thrown it in the cab. The entire ordeal only took a few seconds.

He returned to the ravine and left Mark in the truck's bed. When he first got out of their vehicle, he said, "If you try to escape, I'll have the dogs rip you to shreds, so I wouldn't try that if I were you." He put the dogs in the truck's bed with Mark and then ignored him until it started getting dark. He took the dogs some water while he was waiting for dark.

After it was good and dark, he finally went to the truck and had the dogs jump out. He leaned in at a wide-eyed Mark Silvers and said, "I know you don't know me, but you might remember my twin brother, Dalton. You and your vigilante group killed him not too long ago. Mark, you would've been better off if you'd just stayed out of it. It was none of your business. Now, you'll have to pay for what you did to my brother." Mark still had the tape over his mouth, and Cooper didn't want to hear what he might say anyway. He knew he would try to make up some flimsy excuse as to why he was in the vigilante group in the first place. Cooper was way past listening to anything he might have to say.

Around midnight, he pulled Mark from the truck and dumped him on the ground. Mark had wet his pants, and now he had dirt clinging to the wet spot. Cooper said, "I'm going to cut the tape loose from your legs, but don't try to run because the dogs would love to kill you, especially Dalton's dog Skeeter. We will take a walk back to your hometown of Red Mountain. I'm sure you'll be okay with that. You know the place you love and are willing to kill someone for." He put Mark's hat back on his head.

When they got about halfway to where they were heading, Mark had the bright idea of making a run to escape. Cooper let him run about ten yards before giving Skeeter and Samson the command to attack but not kill. The dogs hit him from behind and knocked him to the ground. They ripped at his face and neck with their sharp teeth for several seconds before Cooper gave them the command to heal. They immediately stopped their attack and stood by his side. Cooper went over to the ripped-up and bleeding Mark and said, "None of that was necessary, Mark; you knew you couldn't outrun two big dogs. Now you're all ripped up for nothing." He picked Mark up and said angrily, "Don't try that again, or the next time, I won't stop the dogs; I'll let them kill you."

He kept Mark, himself, and the dogs hidden as they made the rest of the walk back near the Silver Dollar Saloon without any problems. It was about one o'clock in the morning, and everyone in town had turned out their lights, and it was dark when they arrived. Cooper walked Mark over to the hole of the old mine shaft. He taped Mark's legs together again as he laughed and said to him, "I'm going to throw you down in the mine, but don't worry, if the fall doesn't kill you, the ghosts of that place down there will surely get you after a few days." Mark tried to wiggle himself free, but he couldn't as Cooper shoved him, and he went headfirst into the hole. It only took a few seconds to fall a hundred feet, and he landed with a colossal thud. Cooper then shined his flashlight down on him and saw that his mangled body wasn't moving.

When he finished with Mark, he and the dogs returned to the ravine, got in his pick-up, and returned to the shack.

***

Chapter 15

Cooper was laying low for several days at the shack, not trying to draw any suspicion to himself. The day after he killed Mark Silvers, he got up early in the morning and dug a hole behind where he always parked his truck. Cooper made the hole about twelve feet in diameter and dug every morning, and after, it got dark for several days. Once it got too deep and he couldn't climb out without help, he tied a rope to the back of his truck to pull himself in and out of the hole. He scattered the dirt around so there wasn't a big pile.

Once he had it deep enough, Cooker started taking the dogs into the desert while he looked for some Mojave rattlesnakes. Since they were the deadliest rattlesnakes in the desert, he wanted to collect many of them and put them in the pit. He carried a large empty paint bucket with a lid and a long six-foot rake handle. He made a lasso and attached it to one end of the rake handle to lasso the snakes around the head and capture them.

He spent four days hunting for them, and each day, he would bring what he found back and dump them in the pit he'd dug. When he had about twenty of them, he covered the hole with a tarp he had used to cover the truck's bed. He then threw a thin layer of dirt over it and covered it with limbs of desert bushes so nobody knew it was there.

It took him eleven days of work, and he was now ready to visit Frank Townsend's house in Johannesburg. He waited until it was almost dark before he left the shack with the dogs. When he got to Frank's house, it was dark. The people from Johannesburg weren't familiar with his truck, so he felt safe taking it into town. He drove by Frank's house very slowly, and his car was in the driveway. There was a light in the tiny house's living room, and Cooper believed Frank might be watching something on television, just like Ashley had said. He parked his truck a few blocks from the house and looked around to ensure nobody was watching him as he and the dogs got out.

Cooper had covered his face with charcoal and wore black clothes before going to the house. When he crept to the house, he peeked through the window, and Frank sat in a lounge chair watching television. Cooper slowly turned around to the back and checked the door to see if it was closed. He very gently turned the handle and soon found it was unlocked. The house wasn't massive, so he figured the dogs could be on Frank before he had a chance to realize what was happening.

He told the dogs to get ready and gave them an order. He then knocked on the door with his shoulder, and the door flew open. As soon as he did that, the dogs ran straight for Frank and pinned him down in seconds. He didn't even have a chance to fire the rifle he had grabbed. Skeeter bit down hard on his arm and immediately dropped the gun.

Cooper quickly approached him and told him to sit back down or he would let the dogs finish him off. He slowly followed Cooper's instructions and sat down. Cooper immediately wrapped duct tape over his mouth. He then told the dogs to let him go. He grabbed Frank by the back of the collar of his shirt with both hands and threw him face down to the floor. Cooper wrapped the duct tape around Franks' hands to not get free. He said, "We're going to take a little walk, Frank, and I don't want you to try to run, or I'll have the dogs kill you. Do you understand me?" Frank shook his head up and down.

Cooper walked him back to his pick-up, ensuring nobody was watching. When he arrived, he had Frank lie face-first in the truck's bed. Having him bend his knees and raise his feet toward his back and hands, Cooper wrapped his feet several times with duct tape and then hogtied his feet to his hands. He told Frank, "We're going to take a ride, and it's going to take a little while, so don't do anything stupid. If you try anything, I'll pull over and have Skeeter and Samson rip your throat out."

Once Frank was in the truck, he returned to the shack. They were on the dirt road leading to the hut when Frank decided to try desperately to escape on one of Cooper's sharp turns. When Cooper came to a significant bend in the winding road, Frank managed to roll his body with the turn and flop his body up and out onto the dirt road's side. He was lying there trying to catch his breath when Cooper stopped the truck and approached him. He looked down at him, "What a stupid thing to do, Frank. What did you think you would accomplish by doing that? You're still tied up, you big dummy." He then gave Skeeter and Samson the command to attack but not kill. They ripped on Frank for about thirty seconds before Cooper had them heal. He then picked the bloody Frank up and threw him in the back of the truck again. "Don't do something stupid like that again. The next time, I won't stop the dogs from killing you." When he returned, it was around midnight, and he was tired. He left Frank in the truck's bed with Skeeter and Samson as he went to the shack and slept for a few hours.

Frank was still in the truck with the dogs as Cooper backed it until the tailgate was at the edge of his dug hole. He then took the tarp off the spot, threw it aside, and had the dogs jump out of the truck. Cooper left Frank tapped together, except the tape covering his eyes, and tied a rope around his shoulder. He said to Frank, "I don't believe you know me, but I want you to know who I am. You and your vigilante group shot my twin brother in the back not too long ago at Red Mountain. You shouldn't have done that, Frank." Frank shook his head as if to say it wasn't him that did it. Cooper told him he didn't care who pulled the trigger. Cooper felt they were all guilty just for being part of the group. He lifted Frank's body and pushed him over and into the hole. When his body hit the bottom of the pit, a few of the angry snakes sank their fangs into Frank. As he jerked around a few times, they lashed out and struck him in the face and over several other body parts.

Cooper left Frank in the hole for the rest of that day and again the next day. Frank had died from the snake bites, and his body was already starting to swell. Seeing that he was dead, Cooper pulled Frank's body up and out of the hole and laid it in the back of the pick-up. He checked inside Frank's clothes to make sure none of the snakes came out of the hole with him.

Around midnight, he drove back to Frank's house, quickly pulled his body off the end of the tailgate, and dumped it in front of his house. It wasn't until the following day that the neighbors found his body. He'd already started ballooning up from all the places he'd gotten bitten by the snakes. His round, bald head looked like it was the size of a basketball.

Cooper was pleased with what he'd done as he sat on the couch and thought about it that night. He said, "I let him off too easy. Unlike the other two guys, Frank didn't have to burn or be thrown a hundred feet to death. He just had a few little snake bites, and that was all. I should've been tougher on him." Then he laughed aloud.

***

Chapter 16

Cooper decided to spend time with Ashley to take his mind off killing people for a while. For the next several days, he drove into Ridgecrest and spent daily time with her. They went to a few movies and fast-food restaurants as they had done before, but mostly, they just hung out and spent time with each other.

During one of his visits, she told him he was again big news with the Sheriff's department and the local police for his actions. She told him it was also on the information that Jim Larson had admitted to being part of a vigilante group in Red Mountain. He told the police that his son and the other two guys killed from around the Rand area were also part of the vigilante group he'd set up. He told them that if they looked around the site, they probably would find Mark Silvers' body because he'd been missing for a few weeks and was also a group member.

He told the police everything that happened when the five men had all gone to the Bailey house that day when Dalton's charred body was in the ashes of the old Bailey home. He told them that he and some other men had shot Dalton before throwing himself into the fire. Three men from that vigilante group died in execution-style murders, and the other was missing. He was now scared because he was the only one left of the group. He said he wasn't worried about himself, but he was concerned about his wife's safety. He was begging for police protection for her.

When the Sheriff's department found out about his story, they put Jim Larson in jail for admitting to taking the law into his own hands and shooting Dalton. They set up a police protection unit for Jim Larson's wife while Jim sat in jail and waited for his arraignment. He could've bailed himself out of jail, but he didn't want to. He figured he was safer in prison than at home.

Taking Jim Larson's advice, the law enforcement agencies joined forces and went on a massive hunt for Mark Silvers and anything else they believed might be suspicious. It took several days, but they finally found Mark Silvers and Donald Pickens' decaying bodies at the bottom of the Silver Dollar mine shaft. They also found old bones and skulls of at least two others in the mine.

When Cooper heard what Ashley told him, he became highly agitated and angry that Jim Larson was in jail. Jim was the guy Cooper wanted to torture and kill the most. He was saving him until the timing was right. Ashley got Cooper to relax when she said, "Don't worry about him, Cooper. They won't keep him in jail for very long. He'll be released soon. You have to be patient, and then you can go after him." Hearing her say that made him feel better, and he immediately calmed down. He just had to be patient and wait for Jim to be released.

He continued to visit Ashley at Ridgecrest every day. He bids his time for Jim to get set free so he can go after him. Jim had his wife stay with one of their kids in another state while he was in jail. He correctly believed the killer wasn't after her and would only kill her if she got in his way. With her being gone, it kept her out of harm's way.

It was only a few weeks later that Jim was out of jail. Despite all his pleas to the judge, he was out while waiting for his trial date. The Judge had the Sherriff's department set up twenty-four-hour protection at Jim's home. When Cooper learned about Jim getting out of jail, he was excited. He knew he had to get Jim before the courts convicted him of a crime, and he didn't want him sitting in jail or prison for an extended period. Cooper smiled and said, "I'm going do my civic duty, Jim, and save you from all that pain and suffering. I'm going to torture and kill you before you go back to jail."

When he returned to the shack, he lay on the couch and began planning his strategy to go after Jim. He had to be patient so he didn't get caught. He believed the Sheriff's Deputies would eventually give up their surveillance of Jim's house. He knew they wouldn't do it forever.

Next month, he drove by Jim's house late to check and see if the deputy's vehicle was still out front. He stayed just far enough away so that nobody ever suspected that he had anything to do with the killings. After the fifth week of driving by about three times a week, the deputy's car was gone. He knew they'd given up Jim's protection, and it was time to go after him.

While there, he visited Ashley and told her he wanted her to drop him and the dogs off in Red Mountain late Saturday night. He told her to tell her Mom and Dad they were going on a date so she would be home a little late. He said, "Meet me on the old dirt road that leads to the shack where I can leave my pick-up parked hidden for a few days. Then I want you to pick us up by the old Silver Dollar Saloon at Red Mountain at exactly eleven o'clock on Tuesday evening."

Ashley was excited to be helping Cooper as she jokingly said, "Does that mean we're partners in crime?"

Cooper looked frustrated, "No, you're not involved, Ashley, and if anything goes wrong, you don't know anything about what happened. Is that understood?"

Ashley pouted, "Okay, Cooper, I was kidding anyway. You don't have to get so upset with me."

He pulled her over to him and gave her a big kiss, "I'm not upset with you. I appreciate that you want to help me, but I don't want you to get involved. You're helping me a lot by just dropping the dogs and me off and then picking us up. That means everything to me."

She smiled, "I will drop you off and pick you up on Tuesday, Cooper. You can count on me."

When Saturday rolled around, she met Cooper right when and where he wanted. He had a five-gallon can of gas, a three-foot-long galvanized pipe, an entire roll of duct tape, and a small bag of dog food. He kissed her quickly and had the dogs jump in the back seat as he threw his things in the trunk.

On the way to Red Mountain, Ashley asked him what he would do to Jim Larson. He looked at her and said, "It's better if I don't tell you my plan just in case I get caught and they try to tie you to what I've done."

She knew he was trying to protect her, "Okay, Cooper, if that's what you want, then I'm okay with that."

When they got to Red Mountain, it was around midnight. He had Ashley drive past Jim Larson's house as he and the dogs stayed low in the seat. He saw that Jim's vehicle was in the driveway, and all the house lights were off. Cooper had Ashley drive down past Mark Silvers' house, and everything was dark there too. He had her turn off the lights in the car as he unloaded everything he'd brought. Cooper had the dogs get out and sit next to him. He kissed Ashley and told her he would see her Tuesday night at eleven. She told him to be careful as she started the car and left.

Cooper taped the dog food and the roll of duct tape on Samson's back so he didn't have to carry it. He then made his way to Mark Silvers' house. Once in position, they watched the house for about an hour. Then he crept around the back and broke a window. He took the duct tape and dog food from Samson's back and laid it aside until he went inside. Not seeing or hearing anyone, he raised the window and sent the dogs in first. He gave them the attack command in case someone hid in the house. Once it was safe, he left everything inside the back door. He found a place comfortable on the couch and got as much sleep as possible for the night.

He woke early and started watching Jim's house to see if he could get a glimpse of him. For most of the day, Jim would just come out briefly and then go back in. Whenever he came outside, he carried a rifle and had a pistol stuck inside his belt. Jim looked around in every direction as if looking for someone each time he came outside. Cooper watched him for a few days, and not much changed with him as he did almost the same thing every day.

As soon as it got dark on Monday night and Jim was in bed, Cooper took the five-gallon can of gas, duct tape, and galvanized pipe and crept slowly over to the house. He had the dogs stay low to the ground, pouring three-quarters of the gasoline outside the house and pouring it everywhere except the back door. I put the can aside and went to the back door when I finished. He had the duct tape in one hand and the pipe in the other as he lit the gas on fire, and the house instantly went up in flames. In just a few minutes, Jim came running out the back door just like Cooper had planned. He had his pants and shoes on and his rifle in his hands. He had the pistol in his belt.

As soon as he had a clear shot at him, Cooper stepped out from behind the back door and hit him in the side of the head with the galvanized pipe. He immediately went down to the ground, and while he was down, Cooper tied his hands behind his back with duct tape. Cooper put duct tape over Jim's mouth, picked him up by his belt buckle, and started directing him toward Mark Silvers' house. At first, Jim tried to fight with Cooper, so he hit him again in the head with the pipe. Not enough to kill him, but enough to try and slow him down a little. He also went down, but this time only to his knees. Cooper grabbed him by the buckle again and said, "You try another stunt like that, Jim, and I'll take you back and throw you in that fire. Do you understand me?" He had the gas can and duct tape in one hand and Jim Larson by the belt with the other and headed back toward Mark's house.

Just before they got to Mark's house, Jim tried to break free again and run. This time, Cooper commanded the dogs to attack but not kill. He let them rip at Jim's flesh for about fifteen seconds until he was satisfied. When Cooper picked him up this time, Jim was bleeding from several deep bite marks on his shoulders, head, and face. He laughed, "Man, you are one stubborn old fool. I have you tied up, and I have two dogs that can kill you, and you're trying to run. What are you thinking, Jim?" He guided Jim to the back of Mark's house and quickly pushed him inside. Once in the living room, he pushed him down to his stomach and taped his feet together. He then put tape around his feet and his hands behind his back so he couldn't move.

By then, Jim's house was starting to burn to the ground as neighbors had come over trying to fight the fire. Cooper looked over at the burning house and laughed, "Wow! You should see this, Jim. It's a pretty good show. Your house looks just like a Christmas tree on fire." By the time the fire trucks got there, the house was gone. Cooper just sat and watched it burn and laughed the entire time.

Later, when everyone had left, he went over to Jim and ripped the tape from his mouth. "If you even make a sound without me asking, I'll have the dogs kill you." Jim didn't listen to what he just said and tried to yell out. Cooper repeatedly put the tape over his mouth and had the dogs attack him. After he called the dogs off, he laughed and said, "You're one dumb S.O.B. Jim. You've got to be the craziest and dumbest of all your vigilante friends. You're just plain stupid."

While he lay there bleeding over most of his body from the dog bites, Cooper said, "I guess you know by now that I'm the guy that killed your son and your entire vigilante comrades. I assume you know why I killed all of them. You and your group came to our place and didn't even know if we had done anything wrong. You just assumed we did and started shooting. You shot my brother Dalton in the back; he wasn't even armed. He then threw himself into the fire of our house so you guys couldn't have the satisfaction of retrieving his body. My question to you, Jim, is, why would you shoot someone who isn't armed in the back if you didn't even know for sure he did something wrong?"

Cooper ripped the tape to one side of Jim's mouth so he could talk. He quickly blurted out, "We had a pretty damn good idea. It was you boys that killed our friends."

Cooper said, "That was a huge mistake on all of your parts, wouldn't you say, Jim?"

Jim clenched his teeth and angrily said, "If you take this tape off me, I'll rip you from limb to limb."

Cooper laughed aloud, "Oh, your big stupid dummy, you don't have to worry about that."

Jim yelled, "You're just a crazy psychopath who loves to torture and kill people."

Cooper chuckled and replied, "You're right, but I never would've killed you, your son, and your friends if you would've just minded your own business and let the law take care of things. It wasn't your fight. That's what the law is supposed to do, not people like you and your friends who shoot first and ask questions later. My brother and I were twins, and we did everything together, but you and your friends took all that away from me. I hope you're proud of yourselves for killing an innocent person. My brother never killed your friends,—I did." He then put the tape back over Jim's mouth again. He laughed, "We're going to sit here for the rest of the night and through most of tomorrow, and then we have a Weenie roast, just like I did with Kerry." When he said that, Jim started squirming and trying to get free. Cooper just watched and laughed at him.

Cooper wanted to torture Jim a little more the next day, so he let the dogs attack him twice. After the second attack, he started losing a lot of blood, and Cooper became afraid that he might die before he had a chance to roast him. He lifted Jim's head and said, "Don't you die on me, Jim. We still have our Weenie roast to do. I don't want you to miss that!"

When it was dark enough, he went and got the gas can and poured the rest in it all over Jim's body. Jim was wrenching in pain as the gas hit the fresh dog wounds. Cooper let it soak in well before he had the dogs go outside. He poured gas into a jar, stuffed a rag in it, then went over to the stove and turned on all the gas valves in the kitchen. Leaving the duct tape and gas can near the stove. He stepped out the back door, lit the rag on fire, and threw it on Jim. The gasoline immediately caught fire, went up with a gush, and engulfed Jim and everything around him.

When he reached halfway back to where he was to meet up with Ashley, the house blew up from the leaking gas he'd turned on in the kitchen. He turned around and smiled as he watched a giant ball of flames shoot up in the air.

Ashley waited for him as he and the dogs returned to their meeting place. He opened the back door and let the dogs in; he jumped in and quickly kissed Ashley. "Thanks for being here."

It was almost midnight when they made it back to Cooper's truck. When they got there, he kissed Ashley a few more times and told her he would come to Ridgecrest in a day or so and spend some time with her. They quickly left in opposite directions as he returned to the shack.

***

Chapter 17

Cooper spent a few days at the shack and went to town to see Ashley. He did what he always had done and left Skeeter and Samson in the hut while he went to see her.

It was almost noon when a couple of adventurous dirt bikers camped deep in the desert made their way to the shack. They were camped several miles away, riding their bikes through the desert.

When they first came upon the shack, they were curious about it and made a couple of slow circles around it until they spotted the well. They figured they could get water, so they pulled their bikes over and jumped off. They removed their helmets and yelled hello a few times to see if anyone was around. Not getting a response, one said, "Can you believe this old place way out here in nowhere?"

The other one laughed, "It's crazy. Someone like us must've liked the desert about a hundred years ago." The bikers were in their mid-twenties, in their too-early thirties, and good physical shape.

While one of the bikers was pumping water from the well, the other said, "I'm going to go check out this old place and also the hole in the ground we saw out back."

The other one said, "You go ahead. I'm staying right here. Old places like that freak me out."

When the biker got around behind the house, he walked over to the hole in the ground. That's when he saw the snakes at the bottom of the pit. He momentarily jumped back as he yelled to his friend, "Damn! That's freaky! There must be fifty snakes in this hole."

He then saw Cooper's cut-out in the back of the house he used for a door. By then, his curiosity was getting the best of him, so he decided to peek inside the old shack. He pulled the makeshift door off and laid it to the side. When he did that, he heard Skeeter and Samson's deep, low, and terrifying growls.

When he heard that sound, he panicked and ran for his bike. He didn't put the door back over the hole. He yelled at his friend when the dogs came running out of the Shack after him. They hit him from behind. They knocked him to the ground, but he had biker boots and gear, flipped over on his back, and started kicking and fighting them off as they attacked him. The entire time he was being attacked, he yelled for help from his friend.

His friend saw what was happening, so he quickly put his helmet back on and started up his bike. He then raced the engine to full throttle and took off straight for the dogs. The dogs were so intent on getting the biker on the ground that they weren't paying attention to anything else. He hit Skeeter in the middle of the back with the front tire at about fifty miles per hour. It instantly broke Skeeter's back, and he began yelping and crawling with his front feet toward the shack.

Samson temporarily stopped the biker he was attacking and started chasing the other biker who hit Skeeter. That gave the guy a chance to make it to his feet. Then, he began to run for his bike again. Seeing that he couldn't catch the other guy on the bike, Samson gave up his chase for him and went back on his attack on the guy running for his motorcycle. He was biting at his legs and arms and trying to jump up and grab him by the throat as he chased after him.

The other biker that had hit Skeeter had gone down about fifty yards and turned around by then. Seeing that his friend was still in serious trouble and under attack, he took off again at full speed toward Samson. He hit Samson in the middle of his chest. He struck him with his motorcycle, like running into a huge rock. The biker flew off his bike and landed several feet away on the ground. Samson went tumbling across the floor several times and was severely injured.

That gave the biker just enough time to get to his bike. Seeing that Samson was injured, he started his bike, quickly revved up the engine, and took off at full speed toward him. Samson struggled to reach his feet as the biker hit him hard and ran over him with both tires. Angry and bleeding from being attacked by the dogs, he circled and ran over him a few more times to make sure he wouldn't get up and try to attack them again. The biker ran over Skeeter a few times. He was yelling and cursing the dogs the entire time he ran over them.

Once he thought both dogs were dead, he pulled up on his bike next to his friend and said, "Are you okay?"

His friend replied, "Yeah, I'm fine, just a little shaken up and bruised." He went over and picked up his bike, which had a bent front wheel from the impact of hitting Samson at a fast speed. He pushed it and said, "I think I can still ride it back to camp like that if we go slow." He looked around and said, "We better get out of here before the guy that lives there comes after us with a gun for killing his dogs. You must get bandages for your wounds once we return to camp."

On the way back to their camp, they talked about the dogs' size and how lucky they were to get away without one of them getting killed. The one biker thanked his friend a few times for saving his life.

Cooper didn't get back until later that afternoon from seeing Ashley. When he first pulled up to where he always parked his truck, he immediately saw the door of the shack's back and both dogs lying outside on the ground. Cooper yelled out, "Oh, God, what happened here!" Samson was still breathing, but it was labored, and he was barely alive. Skeeter had died from his injuries before Cooper had gotten back. He went over and picked Samson up in his arms, and he was limp and lifeless. Cooper could tell that his body had received considerable damage. He knew it was just a matter of time before he would be dead. He instantly started yelling and crying out. The dogs had been his constant companions since puppies. He was now feeling the same gut-wrenching emptiness he felt when Dalton died.

A few hours later, Samson took his last breath while Cooper held him in his arms. He couldn't believe that both the dogs were now dead. They had been with him on so many attacks and seemed invincible to him. He wondered how anyone could've been able to do that to both dogs. Finding one of the injured and the other dead was something he never expected, which devastated him.

Once he could stop crying, he started looking around to see what he believed had happened. He saw the dirt bike tracks and thought he had a pretty good idea as he looked around. Now, he was even more rage that bikers had killed his dogs. He got in his truck and went from one direction to another for a few hours, just looking for them.

He did not find any sign of them. He returned to the shack, dug a large hole, and carefully placed the dogs in it. He then said a few words over them before he buried them. It was hard for him as he sat there for the longest time, thinking about how much he would miss them. Now, for the first time, he was all alone.

Not being able to rest, he decided to drive deeper into the desert once it got dark and see if he could spot any campfires. He had gone miles in different directions when he finally spotted a fire. When he made it to their camp, he drove up, and there were the two young men he believed had killed his dogs. They had a pick-up with a trailer to pull their dirt bikes and a tent they had set up to sleep in. Their music was loud, and they drank heavily from a Jack Daniels whiskey bottle.

When he first pulled up, he smiled and acted friendly as he got out of his truck and asked them how things were going. They could tell he was a young guy, so they were familiar with him and said things were good. Cooper went over to where they had their bikes leaned against the trailer and saw the bent wheel on one of them. He said, "What happened to your wheel? It looks like you had a little problem?"

One of the guys laughed and said, "Yeah, we had a little, big dog problem, but we took care of it." Both just laughed.

They didn't offer information about what happened, and Cooper didn't ask. He already knew what they had done. One of the guys offered him some weed to smoke, and Cooper told him he didn't smoke but thanked him for the offer. He told them to be careful because of all the snakes in the desert.

They laughed, and one said, "Yeah, we know we've already killed a couple of them."

He told them to have fun as he returned to his truck and left.

He went about a half-mile away and turned out his lights. The rage over the loss of his dogs was starting to eat him up inside, and he could hardly contain his anger. He turned his pick-up around and slowly drove close to their camp with his lights off. Their music went so loud they didn't hear his truck as he parked it not too far away. He then waited until they were both drunk and had gone to bed.

When he believed they were both asleep, he started his truck and hit the throttle at full speed. He ran through the middle of the tent and over one of the boys. He had caught one of the bikers in his sleeping bag and run over him before he knew what had happened. Cooper felt the tires hit him as the truck bounced twice in the air, and he ran over him with both tires. He quickly made a full-circle turn and went for the tent again. The other biker had made it up and out of the tent and started running. Cooper chased him through the desert for a while before he could finally hit him at full throttle from behind and knock him to the ground. He quickly turned the truck around and ran over him while trying to get to his feet. After running them over, he got out of his vehicle, threw their bikes on the ground, and ran over them a few times.

He was still pumped up and angry as he headed back to the Shack, but he felt happy that he'd found the guys who killed Skeeter and Samson. He was glad he could do the same thing they had done to his devoted friends.

***

Chapter 18

The next day, Cooper was sad, so he went into town to talk to Ashley. When he got there, he told her what had happened to the dogs and said he'd found the guys camped out in the desert and killed them. Ashley was numb to all the bad things that Cooper had to do. It didn't seem to faze her when he told her about killing the two young bikers in the desert. She seemed more upset that Cooper had lost Skeeter and Samson than anything.

He spent the next several days going back and forth to see Ashley and spending time with her. During one of his visits, she told him about other campers finding the two biker's bodies he killed in the desert.

She said, "The Ridgecrest coroner's office found dog teeth marks on one of the guys, and he thought that was a little strange, considering how they had been run over several times and killed by a pick-up truck.

The coroner called in the police chief and told him what he'd found on all the bodies of the people killed around the Red Mountain area. He told the Chief that all the bodies had evidence of significant dog teeth marks on them. Even the ones burned had teeth marks indented into their bones. He told him that he believed the guy who killed all the people there used a big dog or dogs to help him capture and kill his victims.

The following day, the Chief called the Sherriff Department and told the Sherriff what the coroner had found. He told him he needed to let all his deputies know and look for anyone traveling with a large dog or dog.

When Deputy Richard Gilbert heard the news about the big dogs, he immediately told his boss about the young guy he'd talked to in the desert several weeks earlier. He told his boss that the young guy was probably still in his teens, and he had two massive dogs with him.

"I never thought about it because he was such a nice kid. He was at the old Shack in the desert where Charles Staples had kept the young girl captive for several years. He said he was from Ridgecrest and was getting water for his dogs when I saw him. We need to check around Ridgecrest and see if we can find him and his dogs."

The Ridgecrest police alerted a white male driving a pick-up and carrying large dogs. They spent the next few weeks stopping every pick-up that came through town with a large dog traveling with them.

After a few weeks and no luck, Deputy Gilbert returned to his boss and said, "Why don't I take a couple of men with me, and we can go out to that old shack in the desert and see if we spot anything? Maybe that kid was staying there. We can check it out and see if he is." His boss said they had nothing to lose, so they might as well give it a shot. Deputy Gilbert took two deputies with him, and it wasn't long before they were on the minor dirt road heading to the old shack.

When they got there, Cooper was still in town with Ashley. They slowly got out and started looking around the place. They had their weapons drawn but soon found the old shack was empty. They believed someone had been living there, but he was nowhere near.

They found what they believed to be a freshly dug grave and a pit full of rattlesnakes outback. Deputy Gilbert started thinking about how Frank Townsend was bitten all over his body by snakes and dumped at his house. Now, he believed he had found the pit full of snakes the killer used for him.

Deputy Gilbert called his office and gave his boss the news. He said, "We think someone has been living out her boss. He's not here, but you must send a forensic team to dig someone or something up. We found a fresh grave, and who knows what's in it. We also found a pit full of rattlesnakes, and I think it's where Frank Townsend got all his bites."

It wasn't long, and the entire area was crawling with the local police and people from the Sherriff's department. They soon had Skeeter and Samson dug up and lying under a sheet. They were doing fingerprints of the house, but they weren't going to get any to help them in their investigation because Cooper's prints weren't on any police files.

Later that day, after Cooper visited with Ashley, he drove back toward the road that led to the shack. Before he turned into the street, two police vehicles turned onto the dirt road and headed toward the hut with their lights on. Cooper knew they had somehow figured out his hiding place. He kept going straight and headed back to Red Mountain. When he got to the ravine, he drove down and hid for the rest of the night.

The next day, Cooper knew he couldn't stay camped in the ravine forever. He had to have a place where he could sleep at night. He decided to check out his Uncle Tucker's old house and see if anyone lived there.

Once dark enough, he took Charley's truck and headed to Randsburg. He drove by his Uncle Tucker's old house and found it still empty, but it did have a "For Sale" sign out front. He pushed the old pick-up down by "The Joint" and parked it in a secluded spot. He returned to Tucker's house, found a rock, and broke a window in the house's back. He then climbed in and quickly made himself at home.

The water and electricity were still on in the house. He was able to stay there during the nights. He was careful not to turn any lights on to bring any attention to himself. He figured he would return to the ravine during the day, hang out there, and then return to the house at night and sleep.

He stayed at the house every night and then went back to the ravine during the day and continued to do that for about two months. He kept moving the pick-up from place to place so people wouldn't get suspicious. At night, he broke into a few houses around town and could steal enough food to care for himself. He also drove to Ridgecrest and visited with Ashley every chance he could.

His money was getting a little low because most of what he had left was hidden in the Mason jar in the secret hiding place at the old shack. He decided to go back to see if he could get the money. He figured it had been long enough, and law enforcement agencies had probably given up on him ever going back there again.

When he got to the shack that night, he drove around it to see any vehicles. Not seeing any, he parked around the back like always. He took off the little door to the back and slowly went inside. He quickly went to where he'd hidden the money and was relieved that it was still right where he'd left it.

He took the jar and sat down on the couch. He'd only been there a few minutes when he heard a megaphone from out in front.

Deputy Gilbert said, "We surround the place, so you might as well come out now. We'll come in and get you if you don't." Cooper figured he was bluffing because he hadn't seen or heard any vehicles drive up. Deputy Gilbert was bluffing because he was alone, and his truck was parked a little away from the shack. He had hiked back to a spot near the hut, hiding and waiting to see if anyone would appear.

Cooper kept low and quickly ran out to the pick-up and grabbed the five-gallon can of gas he carried as a spare from the truck's bed. He took it back inside the shack and poured the gasoline inside. Cooper grabbed the jar of money and went through the back door opening. On his way out, he lit a match, and the little shack instantly went up in flames.

He quickly jumped in his truck and took off through the desert. Deputy Gilbert was firing his gun at the vehicle as Cooper sped away. When he got to his truck, Cooper was far away from him in the desert. He tried to pursue Cooper but finally got his truck caught upon large rocks during the chase.

Cooper had spent enough time in the desert to find another route back to Red Mountain without taking the minor dirt road. It was a lot slower and tricky in some places, but it was another way out of that part of the desert. By heading west from the shack and then cutting around the mountain's bottom, he could get back onto highway 395. It was a little harder to find at night, but he could return without getting caught by the law.

He drove his pick-up down the ravine and exchanged it for Charley's truck. He returned to Randsburg and his Uncle Tucker's house and tried to relax. He had the money he needed but thought about how close he had come to getting caught. He felt lucky that they didn't capture or kill him. He also felt a little lost and could never return to the old shack that had given him and the dogs so much security and protection.

The next day, he decided to go into Ridgecrest and talk to Ashley to see if she had any ideas for him. He wanted to tell her that the shack was now gone, that he burned it to the ground.

While traveling along the main road toward Ridgecrest, a California Highway Patrol officer pulled in behind him. He was only a few miles from Ridgecrest when the police officer put his lights on Cooper's truck. Cooper said, "Oh man, I don't have a gun or anything to protect myself!" He pulled his pick-up off the side of the road as the officer pulled in the right behind him. He said, "Ok, Cooper, just keep cool and see what this guy wants."

Cooper looked at him from his driver-side mirror as the officer exited his vehicle. He thought the officer looked like he might have been with force for a while because he was in his mid-forties and a little overweight. He figured he could get away from him if they got into a fight.

When he walked up to the pick-up, he had his book out like giving Cooper a ticket. He said, "Hey, son, can I have your license and registration, please?"

Cooper thought, "Man, I'm dead. I don't have either of those things he's asking for." In a deep, accented southern drawl, he said, "I'm sorry, officer, this ain't my truck. It belongs to my dad, and I don't know where the registration is. We just got here from Tennessee, and someone broke into our truck on our way here and stole my wallet with my driver's license and everything. I haven't even had a chance to get a new one from the D.M.V. yet."

The officer said, "Did you know your truck's license tags have expired? That's why I pulled you over."

Cooper said, "No, I didn't know that, officer; as I said, it's my dad's truck, and he takes care of those things."

The officer said, "I'm going to give you a fix-it ticket, and you'll have thirty days to get your tags and license squared away." He then asked Cooper for his name and address, and Cooper quickly gave the officer the name of Cooper King and his Uncle Tucker's Randsburg address.

Everything seemed to be working fine until the officer started to walk back to his vehicle, and a call came in from the radio dispatch. Cooper had already jumped out of the truck and walked back behind the officer when it came in.

The person on the other end of the call said, "The person driving the vehicle is a suspect in the murders around Red Mountain, and he needs to be apprehended. All Cooper heard was that it was necessary to arrest him. As soon as he heard those words, he ran as hard as possible toward the officer. By then, the Officer started to pull his gun out when Cooper hit him like a football lineman tackling a running back. He knocked the officer to the ground, and when he did that, he grabbed the officer's gun.

While lying beside his patrol car, Cooper shot the officer three times from a distance. Two bullets were to the chest, and one hit him in the shoulder. He tucked the gun in his belt, then ran, jumped back in his pick-up, and headed straight to Ashley's house. The officer he shot was wearing a vest, and the two bullets to the chest just temporarily stunned him. The other one ripped a hole in his shoulder.

After a few minutes, he could get back on his feet and radioed for backup. He described the truck that Cooper was driving and the driver. As Cooper got to Ridgecrest and turned off Ashley's road, two police cars came speeding by the street, going in the opposite direction to help the wounded police officer.

When he got to Ashley's house, he ran to her door, beating it wildly. Ashley heard the commotion and came running to see what was going on. When she saw that it was Cooper, she quickly let him in. He was breathing hard and yelling as he told her he had just killed a highway police officer. She tried to get him to calm down enough so she could speak to him. After talking for a few minutes, he gradually regained control of himself.

Ashley's mom and dad had been in the other room when Cooper arrived. Ashley's mom heard him say he had killed a highway police officer, and she immediately ran to the phone in the kitchen and called the local police.

While she was calling Ashley's, Dad went to the vault where his wife kept her weapons and grabbed a 45 pistol. He loaded it and took it with him as he ran into the room where Cooper and Ashley were standing. He stood there with his feet apart and the gun aimed in Cooper's direction.

Cooper froze and pointed the highway patrolman's gun at Ashley's dad. Her dad said in a somewhat slurred speech, "Is this the guy that kidnapped you, Ashley? Is he the one that raped you all those years? If he's the one, I'm going to kill him."

Ashley went over to her dad and calmly tried to talk to him and tell him that Cooper was the one who had saved her, not the one who had hurt her. Cooper had the gun ready to fire as he yelled, "Tell your dad to put down the gun, Ashley, or I'm going to kill him! You need to move away from him, Ashley."

Ashley then told Cooper that her dad was supposed to be watching her the day Charlie abducted her, but he got a phone call and went into the house to talk to someone. When he came back out to check on her, she was gone. He blamed himself for her disappearance, and one day, not too long after she went missing, he put a gun under his chin and pulled the trigger. It didn't kill him, but it left him with brain damage. "He doesn't live here most of the time; he's in a convalescent home. They just let him come visit once in a while." Cooper always wondered why he'd never met her dad and Ashley didn't talk about him. Now he understood why.

Ashley pleaded, "He doesn't understand many things, Cooper. He gets them mixed up. Just put down the gun because I don't want you to kill my dad." Cooper held the gun steady, "I can't do that, Ashley. What if he decides to shoot me once I put it down?"

She said, "Just let me try and talk to him and see if I can get him to give me the gun. He isn't even supposed to have a gun. I don't know where he got it. It must be my mom's."

Ashley tried to get her dad to put the gun down, but he wouldn't. He said to her again that he would shoot him if that were the guy who kidnapped her. She told him that Cooper wasn't the guy. She told him again that she had killed the older man who did that to her. Not understanding what she was trying to say to him, he thought she wanted him to kill Cooper, so he fired one wild round at him. It didn't hit him, but Cooper wasn't sure if he would try it again. He ducked down and told Ashley she needed to get the gun or he would put a bullet in her dad. At about that same time, the police sirens blasted as they came in their direction. Cooper quickly went to the window to look out and see what was happening. Ashley took the gun away from her dad and put it behind her back when he did that. She then went over to Cooper and tried to talk to him.

Cooper started panicking as she raised her arms to calm him down. He didn't know she had the gun in her hand. While hugging him, Ashley looked up at him and told him she loved him as she kissed him. She then quickly put the gun to his heart and pulled the trigger. She held him there for a moment while he was dying, her eyes unseeing and her voice flat and cold as she said, "I had to draw the line there, Cooper. I couldn't let you kill my dad. I know you understand. I'm sorry."

***

Special Thanks

I want to thank my daughter, Danielle Nicole Derby Carter, for helping me with the computer work.

I want to thank my sister, Sharon Duvall, for giving me ideas and editing the book. I am grateful for her support.

Cover Image: SofieLayla Thal via Pixabay

Cover Design: yourebookcover.com

***

Sources of information

Wikipidea – The Free Encycolopidea

***

Other books by Ron L. Carter @ smashwords.com

Twenty-One Months

From the Darkness of My Mind

The American Terrorist: A Grandfather's Revenge

The American Terrorist: The Revenge Continues

American Terrorist – The Silent Killer

Unearthly Realms

Night Crawlers (the original story)

Night Crawlers – The Nightmares Continue

Accidental Soldiers

In Defense of Mankind

Zak Thomas: Monster Hunter

Lost Waters

Love me now Don't wait – Poetry book

Ignited

www.ingramcontent.com/pod-product-compliance
Lightning Source LLC
Chambersburg PA
CBHW021450150726

47989CB00001B/477